THE TAILS OF FREDERICK AND ISHBU

The Case of the Purloined Professor

Marshall Cavendish Corporation
99 White Plains Road
Tarrytown, NY 10591
www.marshallcavendish.us/kids

This book is a work of fiction. Names, characters, places, and incidents are products of the author's imagination and are used fictitiously. Any resemblance to actual events or locales or persons, living or dead, is entirely coincidental.

The following quotes that appear in this book are in the public domain:
p. 7 from *King John* by William Shakespeare
p. 74 from "My Heart's in the Highlands" by Robert Burns
p. 75 from "America the Beautiful" by Katharine Lee Bates
p. 78 from "High Flight" by John Gillespie Magee, Jr.
p. 83 from *Poor Richard's Almanac* by Ben Franklin
p. 83 from "Loch Lomond" Traditional
p. 125 and p. 213 from "Bannockburn" by Robert Burns
p. 138 from "The Badger" by John Clare
p. 175 from "On the Late Massacre in Piedmont" by John Milton
p. 175 from "To a Mouse" by Robert Burns
p. 235 from "Home, Sweet Home" by John Howard Payne

Library of Congress Cataloging-in-Publication Data
Cox, Judy.
The case of the purloined professor / by Judy Cox ; illustrated by Omar Rayyan. — 1st ed.
p. cm. — (Tails of Frederick and Ishbu)
 Summary: Rat brothers Frederick and Ishbu again escape the comfort of their fifth-grade classroom to go on an adventure, this time to help their friend, Natasha, seek her missing father, who is a specialist in the biochemistry of domestic animals.
ISBN 978-0-7614-5544-8
[1. Adventure and adventurers—Fiction. 2. Kidnapping—Fiction. 3. Domestic animals—Behavior—Fiction. 4. Rats—Fiction. 5. Mystery and detective stories.]
I. Rayyan, Omar, ill. II. Title.
PZ7.C83835Cas 2009
[Fic]—dc22
 2008000293

Book design by Vera Soki and Virginia Pope
Editor: Robin Benjamin

Printed in China
First edition
10 9 8 7 6 5 4 3 2 1
Marshall Cavendish

Dedicated to all the fifth graders who have ever asked,
"What do I need to know this for?
When will I ever use this?"

∞ **THE TAILS OF FREDERICK AND ISHBU** ∞

The Case of the
Purloined Professor

by **Judy Cox**

with illustrations by
Omar Rayyan

Marshall Cavendish

CONTENTS

Prologue: A TIGHT SPOT

A rat who gnaws on a cat's tail invites destruction.

—Chinese proverb

FREDERICK AND HIS BROTHER, ISHBU, SNEAKED DOWN A sidewalk in San Francisco's Chinatown. Bursts of firecrackers shattered the air, punctuating the beat of drums and horns. The two rats crept through the crowds of sightseers, weaving between people's legs, dodging feet and wheeled strollers. Every so often, Frederick glanced behind them, searching the crowd.

The night sky was black overhead, but the neighborhood was lit with lanterns. Smoke from the firecrackers mingled with the scent of roasting meat, fresh fish, ginger, and jasmine.

Elaborately decorated floats sailed up the street, followed by marching bands, acrobats, and martial arts groups. Onlookers cheered. Frederick looked back and saw two menacing figures detach themselves from the throng and sprint down the street after them.

"Run, Ishbu!" shouted Frederick.

The rats broke into a gallop. They scurried in and out of the parade, dodging dancers and musicians, zigzagging under the enormous floats.

"I can't make it, Freddy!" cried Ishbu. His breath came in ragged gasps.

"Don't stop!" Frederick yelled back.

Ishbu scrambled after his brother, his fur slick with sweat.

A gigantic golden dragon swayed toward them, its jaws open.

Was this their last chance?

"Follow me!" shouted Frederick.

Without wasting another second, without stopping to check for danger, the two rats dashed straight toward the dragon's yawning maw.

Into the dark. Into the unknown.

Into the mystery.

Part One:
THE CITY

The day shall not be up so soon as I,
To try the fair adventure of tomorrow.
—William Shakespeare

THE ORDINARY WORLD

HOW DID THESE TWO PAMPERED classroom pets get into this tight spot?

Only the day before, Ishbu was napping on the top floor of their comfortable cage in Miss Dove's fifth-grade classroom. He smacked his lips as he dreamed of oatmeal cookie crumbs, stale potato chips, celery sticks with peanut butter, and other bits of leftover school lunches.

On the bottom floor, Frederick pressed his nose against the bars of the cage, ears perked, eyes wide, listening to Miss Dove. Unlike his brother, who had a white coat and "hood" of black fur, Frederick was gray (the color known to rat fanciers as lilac). While Ishbu was plump and fond of food, Frederick was trim and athletic. Both rats had eyes as black as onyx beads and skinny pink tails.

"Now, children," Miss Dove said in her gentle

voice. "Today, we'll finish our aviation unit with the story of two famous pioneers of flight. Charles Lindbergh, known as Lucky Lindy, made the first solo flight from New York City to Paris in May 1927. In those days, the flight took a day and a half. To keep the plane light and to save fuel, Lindy took only four sandwiches with him."

Ishbu stirred. His stomach growled at the thought of going so long on so little food, while Frederick thrilled at the thought of flying solo. *What an adventure that would be!*

Miss Dove continued, "In 1932, Amelia Earhart became the first woman to fly solo across the Atlantic. Even as a child, Miss Earhart was quite the daredevil. When she was eight years old, she built a roller coaster in her backyard using scrap lumber, a packing crate, and roller skate wheels."

Frederick sighed. There was nothing in the whole world that he liked better than listening to Miss Dove. Thrilling tales of explorers! Inventors! Faraway places! In fact, Frederick was so devoted to Miss Dove and her lessons that once—not so long ago—he had traveled halfway around the globe just to be back in her classroom.

Frederick also loved to read. Besides a shoe box filled with fresh fir shavings, Miss Dove always lined the bottom of the rat cage with newspapers and pages from old textbooks.

Ishbu didn't bother with reading or listening. "When are we ever going to need to know that stuff?" he had said more than once.

"You never know when something might come in handy," Frederick always told his brother.

Frederick had hoped Ishbu would change his attitude after their last adventure. But some rats never learn.

When Miss Dove finished her aviation lesson and the children were writing, Frederick scanned the newspaper on the floor of their cage. He wanted to keep up with current events—even if the events were weeks past. "Hey, Ishbu! Come listen to this!" he called.

Although Frederick and Ishbu understood English, they spoke Animal. In addition to grunts and growls, squeaks and snarls, purrs, peeps, barks, moos, and mews, Animal uses silent signals: odors, teeth clicks, tail positions, whisker twitches, eye blinks, ear swivels, and scratching. Rats also use bruxing (grinding their teeth) and eye-boggling (bulging their eyes). So Frederick and Ishbu could carry on interesting conversations (although Ishbu usually wanted to talk about snacks), and Miss Dove and the children heard only an occasional squeak.

Ishbu strolled down the ramp to the bottom floor and leaned over Frederick's shoulder as his brother read aloud:

HEIST NETS FORTUNE IN GEMS

SAN FRANCISCO—Last night a highly organized gang broke into a jewelry store in San Francisco's Chinatown, escaping with thousands of dollars in gems, gold, and pearls, police reported yesterday. "The only clue found at the scene of the crime was the paw print of a dog," said Police Chief Mike Dugan. The police have no leads.

"That's odd," muttered Frederick. "Why would burglars bring a dog?"

But Ishbu (as usual) wasn't listening. Under the article, he'd spotted an ad for some kind of new pet food. He knew it was pet food from the pictures of cats and dogs.

"Boy, oh, boy! I'd love to try this!" he said. "Do you suppose Miss Dove will buy it for us?"

"'Tasty tails pet food—mouthwatering meals for perfect pets,'" read Frederick. There was a picture of a can with a red and yellow label. Frederick peered at the small print along the bottom of the label. "'TTPFCo: made in Switzerland,'" he read. He scratched behind his ear with his hind foot. "Perfect pets," he repeated. "I wonder what that means."

But Ishbu had found a walnut hidden in the bedding and was busy munching.

A VISITOR IN
THE NIGHT

THE FIFTH-GRADE CLASSROOM WAS dark and silent, sliced with shadows from the moonlight that filtered through the window blinds. Miss Dove and the children had been gone for hours. Even the janitor, after mopping the faded green linoleum floors and emptying the overflowing wastebaskets, had left for the night.

Ishbu dozed on the top floor of the cage. His rhythmic snores rumbled peacefully.

On the bottom floor, Fredrick settled down to his evening routine. He dug up a stale peanut from the stash hidden in his bedding to nibble while he read before running laps on his wheel. Without warning, the scent of cinnamon tickled his nostrils like jasmine on a summer night. He knew that scent. . . .

He raised his head—nose twitching, whiskers quivering, ears perked.

And suddenly, *she* was there.

Natasha stood outside the cage, as beautiful as he remembered—long, elegant whiskers, eyes like black pearls, and a coat of glossy lilac fur.

"Tash!" squeaked Frederick. "What are you doing here? I thought I'd never see you again!" He looked closer and saw that Natasha's bright eyes brimmed with tears.

"Frederick," she said, her Russian accent heavy with emotion, "I am coming to beseech you, please. You must be helping me!"

"Help you?" asked Frederick. "Of course! Anything! But how?"

His words woke Ishbu, who bustled down the ramp. "What's going on, Freddy?" he asked, yawning. "Is it suppertime?"

Ishbu stopped when he saw Natasha. "What's *she* doing here?" he asked, his voice frosty. In their last adventure, Natasha had betrayed them; she had redeemed herself in Frederick's eyes by helping them in the end, but Ishbu had never really forgiven her.

Frederick turned to his brother. "That's what I'm trying to find out," he said.

Natasha twisted her tail in her paws. "I come to San Francisco to see my father. Today, it is his birthday. I am to be taking him out to dinner. But when I am arriving at his burrow, he is not there! And his burrow . . ." She stopped.

"Yes, go on," urged Frederick. "What about his burrow?"

Natasha wiped her eyes with her tail and continued. "First I must be telling you—my father is Professor Ratinsky."

"The world-renowned scientist?" exclaimed Frederick. "You never mentioned that before. But I guess we never really had time—"

Natasha broke in. "Yes, he is being quite famous for his work on animal communication."

"Where do you think he's gone?" Frederick asked. "Couldn't he have run out for something? Or maybe he just forgot?"

Natasha shook her head. "Forget his birthday dinner? Never. And his burrow! It has been—how do you say in English? Ransacked!"

"Ransacked?" said Ishbu.

"It means 'scoured,' 'plundered,' 'overturned.' Someone has searched it," Frederick explained.

"But who?" asked Natasha. "I am very much afraid something terrible has happened." Her whiskers trembled.

"He didn't leave a note?" asked Frederick.

"All I find is this empty envelope." Natasha pushed a piece of paper between the bars of the cage. Frederick took it. It was an envelope of heavy ivory paper. He held it to his nose. He couldn't quite place the odor. It smelled unusual, but somehow vaguely familiar.

Frederick turned it over to examine the front.

The envelope was addressed to "Professor Ratinsky, The Burrow, San Francisco, California." In place of a return address, there was a row of Chinese characters. A dragon had been stamped in red ink above it.

"Frederick, you are smartest rat I know besides my father. Help me find him!"

Frederick nodded. "Let's go to his burrow. Maybe we can find clues."

"There may be danger," said Natasha.

Frederick's whiskers curled up. "Ha! I laugh at danger!" He was rewarded with a watery smile from Natasha.

"I knew I could be counting on you, darling Frederick!" She fluttered her silky eyelashes. Frederick blushed to the tip of his tail.

He pushed on the cage door, but it held fast. Frederick's face fell.

"I forgot. Ever since our last trip, Miss Dove keeps our cage locked," he said. The bars were too close together for Frederick to squeeze through, let alone Ishbu.

"Leave all to me." Natasha opened her paw to reveal a slender silver object. Her nail file! It had proved useful once before. . . . Working quickly, she jimmied the latch, and the cage door swung open.

Frederick stepped across the threshold and inhaled

deeply, filling his lungs with the long-untasted air of freedom. His spirits rose. Adventure called—and he, Frederick the brave, would answer!

But Ishbu pulled him back, tugging on his tail.

"Wait, Freddy! Listen to me! Why should we help her? Let's stay here in our warm, cozy cage. We've got food, water, soft beds. No worries. You have Miss Dove and her lessons. No more adventures, Freddy! You promised!"

Frederick looked at his brother. He *had* promised. He nibbled his toenails (a nervous habit he couldn't break). What to do?

On the one paw, there was the beautiful Natasha, clearly in need of his help. Oh, to be a hero once more! Miss Dove's classroom, no matter how cozy, seemed a bit dull once you'd seen the wider world.

On the other paw, after the last time, he had faithfully given his word to his brother that they would stay home.

To go, to follow his heart, to heed the call? Or to stay safe and sound at home?

What should he do?

REFUSAL OF THE CALL

ISHBU DROPPED FREDERICK'S TAIL. "I'm not going, Freddy, and that's final. I'm staying here with my shoe box bed and my carrot sticks. If you want to go, fine. Go. Just don't ask me, that's all." He glared at Frederick for a minute. Then he turned and stomped up the ramp, calling over his shoulder, "Don't wake me up when you come back."

Frederick sighed. It was unlike Ishbu to be so stubborn. They'd been separated only twice since their birth in the pet shop—both times during their past adventure. He'd missed Ishbu's comforting bulk and his good common sense, as steady as a compass pointing north.

But the lure of Natasha's cinnamon scent and the fresh breath of a new quest were simply too strong to resist.

"Good-bye, brother!" called Frederick sadly. "I'll

see you soon!" He stepped outside the cage to follow Natasha.

"Hurry," she said, her tail twitching impatiently.

Together they raced across the classroom floor and swarmed up the radiator to the windowsill. The window was open the tiniest crack, but it was enough for a rat. Frederick followed Natasha through the narrow opening and jumped down lightly into the rose bed.

Leaving Wilberforce Harrison Elementary School behind, the two rats raced up shadowy, winding streets until they reached the top of one of San Francisco's many hills. Frederick stopped to rest. Below him, the lights of the city spread out like a diamond necklace.

He marveled at the view. The moon shone softly on the bay, silvering the waves. The odor of eucalyptus trees filled the night, nearly overpowering the delicate scents of early spring—daffodils and cherry blossoms.

Despite the beauty around him, Frederick shivered. Nighttime isn't safe for pocket-sized prey animals, and he knew it. Besides cats, dogs, ferrets, hawks, owls, snakes, bobcats, and wolves, there were also humans with brooms, traps, poison, and BB guns.

A sharp nip from Natasha got him moving, and they raced onward again, finally stopping in front of a hole concealed between the gnarled roots of a juniper tree.

"My father's burrow," Natasha whispered.

Sniffing for danger, Frederick approached the entrance warily. What would they find inside?

NO CLUE

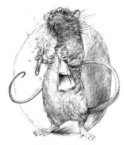 WITHOUT PAUSING, NATASHA DISAP-
peared through the hole. Frederick
glanced quickly around, checking
for enemies lurking in the shadows.
Seeing none, he wriggled through
the hole after her.

The hole opened into an earthen burrow. Frederick
wrinkled his nose, and his fur bristled at the stench.
A dim memory troubled him, something from the
pet shop where he and Ishbu had been born. Looking
around, a terrible sight met his eyes: overturned
tables, torn papers, stuffing ripped from chair
cushions, and shards of broken crockery.

Frederick could see that Professor Ratinsky's
burrow must have been a snug place. But now it
looked as if it had been trashed by a tornado. What
clues could they possibly find in this mess?

Frederick lifted a pile of books from the floor and
set them on the shelf, taking note of the titles as he

did so. Fiction, poetry, history, scientific works. The professor must be a well-read rat. Some of the books were in foreign languages.

"Your father can read all these languages?" he asked Natasha.

"Yes," she said. "Russian, Mandarin Chinese, English, Italian, German, French, and Punjabi. He was born in laboratory in Russia. He immigrated to United States in luggage of graduate student studying at university. There he meet my mother. When I am being little, he teaches me and my brothers and sisters to read. He would nip our tails if we are not practicing enough." She gave a fleeting smile.

Frederick could read—but only English—and he knew very few animals that could read at all. Even his own parents couldn't read. Frederick had learned a few years ago when Miss Dove's fifth graders had partnered with a first-grade class to help them practice reading aloud. One pair of students, Barnaby Hubbard and his first-grade reading buddy, Kitty Swenson, always sat next to the rat cage. Frederick watched and listened, and as Kitty learned to read, Frederick learned, too. He practiced every night, carefully deciphering the words in the newspapers and book pages that lined his cage, while Ishbu napped upstairs.

And one day, like a miracle, Frederick found he could read all by himself. It was like a cage door swinging open—the tremor of excitement, the thrill of achievement, the anticipation of starting a journey.

Imagine being able to read in all those languages!

Natasha's sigh pulled Frederick back from his thoughts. "Where can my father be going without telling me? And why this?" She gestured at the mess with her paw.

Frederick set upright a table cleverly built out of walnut shells. "It looks like someone was searching for something. Is anything missing?"

"So hard to be telling," said Natasha. She surveyed the room. "Some things are gone, I am thinking. His gold pen. And a pair of silver candlesticks . . ." Her gaze stopped on a display case on top of the desk. "Oh, no!" she cried.

"What is it?"

"The Benevolence Medal is gone! It is my father's prize possession. Awarded by the society of something or other—I forget."

"Is it valuable?"

"I suppose. My father was proud just to be honored for his work. Look. Here is picture of him at ceremony in Edinburgh last year." Natasha handed Frederick a framed photograph.

He picked up a magnifying glass from the desk and squinted through it to make out the details. An elderly rat with spectacles perched on his graying snout smiled broadly, showing worn teeth. He held the medal in his paws—a gold star dangling from a navy and white striped ribbon. Each point of the star was crowned with a pearl. In the center of the medal was a map of the world made of inlaid gemstones. There was minuscule writing engraved around the edge of the map. Frederick peered closer, slowly spelling out the letters. "*A bob.* What does that mean?"

"A.B.O.B.," corrected Natasha. "But I am not remembering what it stands for." She touched the picture gently, her eyes clouded.

Frederick handed the photograph back to Natasha. He rubbed his ears and surveyed the burrow. *Would any rat willingly leave his home in such a state? Or was the professor the victim of foul play?*

Natasha tidied up a pile of loose papers. She gasped and waved a piece of paper at Frederick. "See here," she urged. "This must be what is coming in that envelope!"

Frederick took the paper. It was a note, written on ivory paper and stamped with a red dragon. He read the note aloud:

February 16

My Dear Friend,

    It's been ages since we've talked, but I've been following your research with much interest. I think I have some ideas regarding your formula.

Meet me at the Red Dragon restaurant in Chinatown tomorrow at 6:00 p.m.

Sincerely,

Dr. Martin G. Liu

"What research? Who's Dr. Liu?" asked Frederick. "And the letter has yesterday's date on it. Do you think your father might be in Chinatown tonight?"

"Instead of with me at his birthday dinner?" Natasha said doubtfully. "I do not know what this note means, but I can be finding out."

She pulled a chemistry book from the shelf and extracted a thin, black address book from between the pages.

"My father is always hiding things in books," she said. "I tease him about it. It is good thing I know where to be looking." She opened the address book and ran her paw tip down the entries. "Dr. Liu lives not too far. I will go see him."

"I'll stay here and keep searching," said Frederick. "There may be something we've missed."

"Meet me later," said Natasha, "at Good Fortune Herb Shop in Chinatown. Shop is safe place for animals. A friend of mine is staying there. I know he will help." She gave Frederick directions.

The rats brushed whiskers, and Natasha scampered out the hole. Frederick gazed after her for a few seconds. Then he turned back to search the rest of the burrow.

He had taken only a few steps into the next room when he saw—pressed into the dirt floor—the paw print of a gigantic hound!

ISHBU TO THE RESCUE

 MEANWHILE, ISHBU WAS HAVING troubles of his own.

After Frederick left, he'd been unable to get back to sleep. Instead, he fretted all night long, anxiously nibbling the envelope Natasha had left behind.

This was all *her* fault. If she hadn't come . . . oh, why had he ever let Frederick go without him? Frederick was brave, strong, and smart, but even he might run into a jam. And here he, Ishbu, was sitting pretty in their cage, letting his brother charge into danger alone!

Daylight came, and Frederick didn't return.

Ishbu paced back and forth on the top floor of their cage. What could have happened? He'd expected Frederick to return before dawn. The classroom door opened, and Ishbu ran to the bars. His tail drooped when he saw that it was only Miss Dove and the fifth graders.

"Children," said Miss Dove after she had taken roll and conducted the flag salute, "we're running late this morning, so let's move along. We'll start with current events. Who wants to share?"

Ishbu watched halfheartedly as Elias Fischer raised his hand and walked to the front of the classroom. Frederick was the one who liked to hear the news reports. "An educated rat stays on top of world affairs," Frederick said. So now, even though he was upset, Ishbu tried to pay attention. Freddy would want it that way.

Elias Fischer held a newspaper clipping in his hand. "I got this article from *The Chronicle*," he announced. He read aloud:

PET OWNERS PUZZLED

SAN FRANCISCO—Officials remain mystified as unusual behavior in family pets has been reported throughout the city. Cats and dogs sit staring into space, apparently hypnotized. The strange behavior doesn't appear to last long. "I've never seen Prince act like this," said one dog owner, Mrs. Green of Van Ness Avenue. "He wouldn't obey me all afternoon. I couldn't even get him to come inside." Local vets have reported hundreds of calls from worried pet owners but offered no explanation. Investigators are researching connections between the pets, including their food.

Ishbu's ears perked up. Pet food? Now why did that ring a bell? How he wished Frederick were here! If anyone could solve a mystery, Freddy could.

But the hours passed, and Frederick didn't return.

All morning, Ishbu ran back and forth along the bars of his cage until he'd worn a path in the bedding. What should he do? Stay home and wait? Or go after his brother?

Finally, Ishbu decided. Even though he hadn't wanted any part of this new adventure, hadn't wanted any part of Natasha or her problems, he was going.

Once he'd made up his mind, Ishbu prepared quickly. Not for nothing had he once traveled halfway around the world! He scrubbed his ears and groomed his whiskers. (Clean ears and whiskers were better for tracking.) He took a long, long drink of clear, refreshing water from the bottle that hung on his cage. Rats can survive for days without food, but just in case, he gobbled an extra big snack. Because who knew how long it would take to find his brother?

Ishbu realized he wasn't the tracker Frederick was; his nose wasn't as sharp, and—let's face it—he was a tad out of shape. But he was, after all, a rat, with a rat's keen sense of smell, and they'd had no rain last night.

He was certain he'd be able to trace Natasha's unusual cinnamon scent as well as his brother's familiar odor. Pretty sure. Mostly, anyway.

Ishbu would have preferred to wait until night, but he wanted to track while the scent was fresh. So when Miss Dove took her class outside for recess —even though it was daylight, even though he'd never in his life done such a thing on his own before—Ishbu pushed open the unlocked cage door.

He crept out. The room was empty. He fled across the linoleum floor, zigzagging like a quarterback. When he reached the radiator below the window, he stopped to catch his breath.

Suddenly, he heard the click-clack of Miss Dove's heels. She was coming back!

"My goodness, it's chilly this morning!" Miss Dove said. She crossed the floor to the window, her shoes tapping with each step.

Ishbu ducked under the radiator.

"Who left this open?" With a loud thump, Miss Dove slammed the window shut, cutting off Ishbu's path.

Doomed to failure before he even got outside!

THINKING IT THROUGH

FREDERICK SAT NEXT TO THE PAW print, his head spinning. He remembered the Sherlock Holmes stories Miss Dove read to her class: Here was a clue straight out of *The Hound of the Baskervilles*!

Hounds! Canines! Dogs! Fearsome ancient enemies of rats. He forced himself to examine the paw print again, like an observer, like a scientist, not like a puny, helpless rat. On second view, he could see the print wasn't so very gigantic (except to a rat).

Miss Dove always advised her fifth graders to think a problem through. "A pinch of planning at the beginning saves hours of work later," she told them. Of course, she was talking about arithmetic problems, not disappearing rats, but even so. . . .

He wished Ishbu were here. Ishbu wasn't good at thinking problems through, but he was nice to have around while Frederick thought aloud. All alone, Frederick talked to himself.

"What do we know so far?" He counted the clues off on his paw tips. "One: The professor disappeared without notifying his daughter. Two: Someone searched his burrow. Three: Valuable things have been stolen—the professor's medal, his gold pen, silver candlesticks. Four: There's a note from Dr. Liu that may or may not have something to do with this strange business. Five . . ." He stared at the paw print and shrugged. Where did a paw print fit in? And that familiar yet unsavory smell? Nothing made sense.

Time to find Natasha and compare notes. Maybe she had learned something to add to the equation.

Frederick gave a last glance around the burrow and scuttled up through the hole. He popped out, blinking against the sudden brightness, surprised to see daylight. He'd been gone all night! Miss Dove and the children would be worried when they discovered he was missing. And poor Ishbu must be frantic.

His heart gave a painful twist as he thought of Ishbu. But really, Frederick knew he could travel faster alone. At least Ishbu was out of harm's way in their cage. Frederick wished he could let Ishbu know where he was going, but he couldn't spare the time to run home, and he couldn't risk approaching the school in daylight, not with hundreds of eagle-eyed children around! No. First, he would help Natasha find her father. Then he could return, triumphant, to Ishbu and Miss Dove.

The morning fog was burning off, but the lower slopes of the hills were still wreathed in white. The towers of the Golden Gate Bridge poked above the fog like orange steeples. Across the bay, a foghorn blared.

Over the smell of wet juniper and eucalyptus, Frederick could still catch a whiff of cinnamon—and the same rank and unpleasant smell from the burrow. He pushed it out of his mind for now, put his nose to the ground, and followed Natasha's scent.

No Exit

ISHBU COWERED BENEATH THE radiator, shaking like a mouse. Above him was the closed window. Across the room, Miss Dove blocked the door like a guard, greeting her loud and sweaty students as they bustled in after recess.

There had to be some way out. Some way past Miss Dove and her students, some way to reach Frederick. But how?

Ishbu kept watch from his hiding spot. Shoes crossed his view—boots, sneakers, Mary Janes. And the noise! High up in his cage, he'd never noticed how much noise children made just walking to their desks. Footsteps, as loud to Ishbu as a giant's, rattled the floor.

Slam! Miss Dove shut the door firmly behind the last child. No exit! Not from the window, not from the door! Ishbu wrung his paws. He had to get out of

Wilberforce Harrison Elementary School. And fast! Frederick's life might depend on it!

"Now, children," said Miss Dove, "please take out your arithmetic books and turn to page one hundred fifteen." The class raised the lids on their desks and pulled out their faded red textbooks.

When the children were quietly working, Bobby Taylor raised his hand. "Can I have a pass for the restroom, Miss Dove?" he asked.

"*May* I have a pass, Bobby," Miss Dove corrected him. She handed Bobby a pass.

Lost in his thoughts, Ishbu nearly missed his chance. The squeak of the opening door caught his attention as Bobby left the room. Ishbu tensed. This might be . . . if only, if *only* . . . He measured the distance from the radiator to the door and prayed no one was watching.

Bobby had left the door open a few inches. "Go!" Ishbu muttered to himself. He sprang into action, racing along the baseboard, a black-and-white streak. Under the chalkboard, around the first corner, past Miss Dove's desk, behind the wastebasket, around the second corner, toward the door . . .

"Miss Dove!" cried Lisa Lamb. "The rats are out!" She stood by the cage, pointing to the open door.

"Not again," said Miss Dove with a sigh. She clapped her hands to get everyone's attention. "Everybody look. Let's find them quickly, please!"

The children leaped out of their seats and crawled around the floor, calling, "Here, Ishbu! Here, Frederick!" (Hunting for escaped rats was a lot more fun than arithmetic.)

Ishbu didn't dare stop. He hugged the wall and galloped toward freedom.

"Frank!" called Miss Dove. "Shut the door so the rats can't get into the hall."

Frank ran to close the door. Ishbu was nearly there. He saw Frank's high-top sneakers. Just a minute more . . . His lungs burned with the effort. The door was closing. . . . He slid through the gap like a runner into home plate. *Safe!*

Not quite. As Ishbu sat panting in the hall, footsteps echoed down the corridor. He looked up, wide-eyed. A tall, broad figure came toward him, pushing a wheeled cart and—horror of horrors! —carrying that instrument of torture all rats fear and despise: a *broom*.

AN ALLEY IN CHINATOWN

FREDERICK REACHED CHINATOWN in the late afternoon, following Natasha's directions. He'd never been to this fascinating part of San Francisco before. How he wished he could spare a moment to sightsee! The main street was crowded—people shopping, talking, and taking pictures; there were just too many humans for a small animal to feel safe. He dodged into the first alley he came to. This was the most dangerous time of day for a rat to be out, and he wasn't taking any chances.

As soon as he entered the alley, the street sounds faded. Although the alley appeared to be deserted, Frederick darted from one spot to the next—hiding beneath a discarded newspaper, ducking under a garbage bin, skirting a pile of bricks.

A wooden fence ran along one side of the alley.

On the other side, brick buildings bristled with wires, antennas, pipes, and fire escapes as delicate and strong as metal spider webs. He eyed possible hiding places in case he needed one in a hurry.

The concrete under his paws was laced with cracks. He held up his tail so it wouldn't drag through the cigarette butts and trash that littered the alley. Graffiti was scrawled on the walls. Frederick was glad to see pale sunshine break through the thin clouds. This wasn't a place where he'd want to linger after dark.

Back doors stood open, and he could tell by the scents what kinds of stores he passed: noodle shop, fish market, fortune cookie factory, grocery, beauty salon, florist. Signs above each door were written in Chinese characters. Sounds drifted out, too . . . snatches of music and voices. It felt strange not to be able to understand the speech or to read the signs.

Frederick didn't smell any trace of herbs, yet he knew that the Good Fortune Herb Shop was nearby.

He sidled along, close to the buildings, out of sight. Over the medley of aromas, Frederick picked up a whiff of something new—a powerful and nasty smell. He wriggled his nose in disgust. The same odor as at the professor's burrow! He recognized it now. The pet shop where he'd been born had been full of that stink. Dog!

WHAT HAS FOUR WHEELS AND FLIES?

OUTSIDE MISS DOVE'S CLASSROOM, with the janitor (and his broom) bearing down on him, Ishbu searched frantically for some-place to hide. The hallway stretched before him as vast as the Sahara. The classroom doors on either side were closed. Down at the very end of the hall, a rectangle of yellow sunlight streamed through the open front door.

Could he reach the door before the janitor reached him? Rats are good sprinters, but they have no stamina for the long haul, and Ishbu was tuckered out. Two feet away, he spotted a brown paper lunch bag some child had dropped. He raced toward it and dove inside.

The janitor whisked the bag up with one hand and ran the broom along the baseboard with the other. Then he tossed the bag into his cart.

Inside the bag, Ishbu was surrounded with the

tantalizing smell of a peanut-butter-and-grape-jelly sandwich. In spite of his fear and the morning's close calls, his stomach growled. He scrabbled around in the folds of the bag, but the sandwich was long gone; no doubt some child got too hungry to wait for lunch. Nothing left but the smell. He found a few overlooked sunflower seeds and chewed them up. It felt like hours since he'd left Miss Dove's cage.

Only a faint light filtered through the bag, and Ishbu could feel the cart bump down the hall as the janitor rolled it, the wheels clattering across the linoleum. The motion made him queasy. He soon wished he hadn't eaten those seeds.

A door creaked open. The light changed, and a wave of cool, fresh air filled the bag. Even the smells were different—asphalt instead of pencil shavings, eucalyptus instead of library paste.

The motion stopped, and the whole cart tipped upside down. Ishbu and his bag somersaulted through the garbage like a sock in a dryer. He landed on something soft and squishy. In the silence that followed, he heard the janitor roll the cart away.

Ishbu hastily nibbled a hole in the side of the bag and tore his way out. He sat up and peered around. Just as he suspected! He was in the big garbage bin on the edge of the school playground. He'd landed on a bunch of squished grapes.

Wonderful! Now all he had to do was jump out

of the bin and find Frederick and Natasha's trail. Piece of cake! He bruxed happily as he pictured telling Freddy about his escape. Wouldn't his brother be surprised at Ishbu's courage! His cunning! His daring!

But before Ishbu could scramble out of the bin, an enormous garbage truck rumbled up. Ishbu could feel himself being lifted and dumped with the rest of the bin's contents into the back of the truck. Then off it drove.

Trapped again!

LOST

ISHBU RODE IN THE GARBAGE TRUCK all day long, up and down the twisting streets of San Francisco. Fortunately, there had been plenty to eat. Unfortunately, he got quite sick. After a while, he'd fallen asleep in a heap of coffee grounds.

Now, in the slanting light of late afternoon, he yawned, rubbed his eyes, and rolled over onto a mound of moldy grapefruit rinds. He sat up and felt more than a bit muddled. He nibbled a rind unhappily. *If only Freddy were here!*

The truck slowed to a stop. Ishbu's tummy sloshed, his head throbbed, and the garbage (which earlier had smelled enticingly ripe) stank. He was sure he was going to be sick. Again. He'd had enough of adventure, enough of travel, enough of garbage trucks. He wanted to be on steady ground.

The heap of refuse tilted as Ishbu heard the

garbage men climbing aboard. Ishbu knew he had to hurry. He slipped down a pile of banana peels, through the spokes of a broken bicycle wheel, and over a mildewed sneaker. As the truck shifted into first gear, Ishbu grabbed hold of a shoelace and rappelled over the side.

It was a daring act. The sort of athletic feat Frederick always carried out so well. Ishbu landed flat on his back on the road. His bones ached from the impact. He picked himself up and brushed off a bit of peach peel still clinging to his fur.

He wrung his paws. He had no idea what part of the city he was in. He smelled rotting fish and salt air. Seagulls squealed overhead, and somewhere machinery whined and crunched. He must be down by the docks somewhere. The street beneath his paws was paved with crumbling brick. Abandoned wooden buildings leaned tipsily, their faded paint curling up in strips. Wisps of afternoon fog blew in from the bay, and a bitter breeze ruffled Ishbu's fur. Crooked shadows reached for him from every corner.

A couple of wharf rats loped down the middle of the street, as bold as kings. Ishbu eyed them anxiously, but they took no notice and were soon out of sight. The street was deserted once more.

Ishbu sucked the end of his tail for comfort. Miles from home. Alone. Lost in a bad part of town. What had he gotten himself into? He stifled a whimper.

"Hey, you!" a voice growled behind him.

Ishbu turned around. "Who, me?" he squeaked.

A tough-looking ferret stood in the street. "You're coming with us," he said. Two more scruffy ferrets flanked him like soldiers.

Ishbu tried to run, but the chase didn't last long. The ferrets grabbed his legs, pinning him to the ground. The last thing Ishbu saw was a huge paw raised to strike.

IN THE DEN
OF DRAGONS

"HE'S WAKING UP, BOSS," SOME-
one growled.

Ishbu opened his eyes. Ooh,
his head ached! He peered
blearily around. He was lying
on a thick Oriental rug in an
elegant room. The walls were paneled with dark
wood and hung with silk tapestries embroidered with
red and gold dragons. Two husky ferrets guarded the
door. The only light came from a flickering lantern,
but it was enough to hurt his eyes, so he closed them
and let his nose do the work.

He smelled strong, enticing scents—like the ones
on Natasha's envelope—spices and vinegar, soy sauce
and ginger. He sniffed again, and memory swept over
him.

Miss Dove sometimes brought her lunch to
school in a white box with a wire handle. He and
Frederick shared the leftovers—food so appetizing

that they chewed up the cardboard box to get every last morsel. Chinese food! But why did he smell that here?

Ishbu tried to rub his throbbing head, but he couldn't move. He was bound paw and foot! As he struggled, the ferrets snickered.

"So, Mr. Ishbu, again I find you meddling in my affairs."

Ishbu recognized that throaty purr! He opened his eyes.

A huge albino opossum sat enthroned like an emperor in a carved, high-backed chair. His sightless eyes glowed like moonstones, and his head moved back and forth as he talked, sniffing the air. One massive paw held a white-tipped cane.

The Big Cheese! Ishbu and Frederick had encountered the evil criminal mastermind, and his vicious gang known as the Bilgewater Brigade, once before. The possum smiled, but Ishbu wasn't fooled. Goose bumps crawled across his skin.

"Let us have no games," the possum continued. "I want the girl rat, and I want her now. No puny pets will stand in my way, not you or your brother. Do we understand each other?"

The Big Cheese leaned forward. Light glittered off his fifty sharp yellow teeth, and Ishbu winced. "Where is she?" the possum demanded, thumping his cane on the floor.

Ishbu shook his head, too scared even to squeak.

"How unfortunate," the Big Cheese snarled. "Perhaps we can improve your memory." He signaled the ferrets. "Take him away!"

THREE TIMES IS
A PATTERN

FREDERICK SCOOTED UNDER A metal trash bin, afraid to make a sound. His hackles rose as a dog trotted into sight.

It was a *rat terrier*! The very name struck terror in any rat. Rat terriers were efficient and cold-blooded killers.

The terrier stopped a few feet from Frederick's hiding place, so close that Frederick could have counted every one of the dog's brown spots. He watched the dog snuffle the pavement, afraid his ratty scent would betray him. But the street held many odors, and the dog only wrinkled his nose and sneezed twice. The terrier glanced behind him, as if to be sure he wasn't being followed, and then slipped inside an open doorway.

Frederick knew he should find the herb shop and meet Natasha, but the dog's furtive behavior made his whiskers prickle. He recalled the mysterious paw print inside the professor's burrow. Not many breeds of dog can fit into the tunnel of a rat's burrow, but a rat terrier could.

Frederick edged out of his hiding place. *Just a quick peek*, he decided, *to see where the dog went.*

A sign hung above the door. Frederick recognized the picture underneath—a red dragon.

Miss Dove had always taught her fifth graders to pay attention. "Once is an accident, twice is a coincidence, but three times is a pattern," she told them.

This was the third time Frederick had seen that dragon. Once on the envelope. Once on the note. Now this. *A pattern.*

The Red Dragon restaurant. The same restaurant where Dr. Liu had invited Professor Ratinsky to meet him.

Frederick slipped through the open door.

POKER-PLAYING DOGS

 THE DOORWAY IN THE ALLEY OPENED onto a landing. Frederick saw a couple of closed doors and a flight of stairs leading to below street level. He followed the dog's scent down the stairs, keeping watch for trouble. At the bottom was an empty passage paved with brick.

Noises came from a room above him. Rapid voices, speaking Chinese. Footsteps. Water running. The clash and clang of pots and pans. A heavy, rhythmic thudding like a knife chopping on a wooden board. Frederick's long nose wiggled, and the delectable odor of food—the tang of fish, the aroma of roasted meat—filled his nostrils. He must be in the basement of the restaurant. But where was the dog?

A lantern shaped like a pagoda gave off a faint light. Frederick scuttled along the brick passage, staying close to the wall so he could use his whiskers to guide his way. His claws scrabbled against the floor, but far too quietly to alarm anyone. He passed a few doors, each tightly shut. There was no way to tell what lay behind them. Storerooms? Stairs to other shops? More passages?

One door stood half open. Frederick crept close, counting on the aromas from the restaurant to disguise his scent. His tail switched nervously like a cat's as he looked inside.

Two short-haired terriers sat at a table playing cards. The stench was almost overpowering.

"You gonna deal or we gonna sit here all day?" snapped a white terrier with black spots.

The other terrier shuffled the cards. He was the brown-spotted dog from the alley. Both dogs had the same trim build, cruel eyes, and pointed teeth. Both wore red collars.

"No cheating this time," warned the brown-spotted dog as he dealt. "You know you like to cheat."

"So do you. See anything when you was in the alley, Snarl?"

"Nah." Snarl picked up his cards. "Of all the boring jobs, we get stuck guarding the prisoner. Whatdaya say we have a little fun with him, Snip? Show that dirty rat how dogs like to play."

Snip tossed a poker chip into the center of the table. "Nah," he said. "Boss's orders."

"What's that supposed to mean?" asked Snarl.

The black-spotted terrier took a swig of ginger ale. "It means we keep him tied up in the storage room and we wait."

The prisoner they're talking about could be Professor Ratinsky, Frederick thought. *Did these terriers kidnap the professor?*

Snarl tossed a poker chip onto the table. "Ya gotta hand it to the boss. Who else has a network like this? Swanky new digs. Spies everywhere."

Snip laughed—not a pretty sound. "He's gotta paw in every pie, all right."

"Who says crime don't pay?" said Snarl. "When he takes over, we'll be top dogs! Long live the Bilgewater Brigade! Long live the Big Cheese!" The two terriers clinked their ginger ale bottles together and drank.

Frederick stifled a gasp. The Big Cheese was behind this! He should have known! The dogs must have the professor tied up somewhere nearby. He needed to find him and get out of here!

HOUNDED

 FREDERICK SNEAKED PAST THE room and padded stealthily down the passage, pausing at each closed door to sniff and listen.

A faint moan came from behind the last door in the passage. The door was not quite shut, as if someone had closed it in a hurry without checking to make sure it latched. Obviously, the dogs weren't expecting a visitor.

Frederick pushed the door slightly wider with his snout. The room was a closet. Facedown on the floor was a figure bound so tightly with rope that it looked like a cocoon.

"Professor?" Frederick called softly. The only answer was another moan.

Frederick smiled as he imagined Natasha gratefully thanking him for rescuing her father and the Big Cheese's anger when he learned of the professor's escape. He pulled himself together. It wouldn't do to underestimate Snip and Snarl. Just because the dogs were careless didn't mean they weren't dangerous.

Frederick nosed himself into the room. He struggled to untie the ropes binding the rat, but they were too thick. Too bad he didn't have Natasha's nail file. Wait—he didn't need a nail file! He gnawed the ropes with his sharp teeth and was rewarded as they snapped with a twang. The prisoner rolled over and sat up.

Frederick knew that long, wriggling nose! He knew those shoe-button eyes! And that familiar, well-loved smell!

It wasn't Professor Ratinsky! It was—

"Ishbu!" Frederick cried.

"Freddy!" answered Ishbu.

The rats rubbed noses and clicked their teeth happily.

"What are you doing here?" whispered Frederick. He sniffed Ishbu's fur, catching a whiff of garbage. "Phew! Wherever you've been, you need a bath."

Ishbu spit into his paws and started to swab his ears, but Frederick stopped him. "Not here. This place is crawling with spies."

The room had no windows. The only way out was back down the passage to the stairs. *Past the dogs.* "Keep quiet," murmured Frederick. "We can talk later, after we get out of here. Stick close to me."

The two rats sidled through the doorway. Creeping close to the wall, they scuttled down the passage. They could hear the dogs still playing cards.

"We have to get by them," whispered Frederick. "I'll go first." He signaled Ishbu to wait and, with his belly pressed against the floor, he slithered past with no problems. On the other side of the doorway, he stopped and beckoned to his brother.

Ishbu began to crawl, but his tail caught under his paws, and he stumbled. A slight sound, but dogs have keen ears.

"What's that?" growled one of the terriers.

"C'mon. Let's check it out," said the other.

"Run, Ishbu!" shouted Frederick. The rats dashed through the passage and up the stairs toward the outside door, with the dogs on their tails. But the door to the alley was now shut.

Abruptly, a boy in a white apron opened another door on the landing. Frederick and Ishbu sped between his legs. The furious dogs charged after them.

The rats had no time to consider the vast stainless steel cooking range, the walk-in cooler, the people in white caps and aprons. But their noses told them all they needed to know—the restaurant kitchen!

"Hey! What's going on?" yelled a man in a chef's hat, with a huge fish in one hand and a gleaming cleaver in the other. "Get those dogs out of my kitchen!" He hadn't noticed the rats yet.

The dogs ignored the man. Frederick and Ishbu sprinted under the table and along the wall, hoping to find someplace too narrow for the dogs to enter. One of them—Snip, or maybe it was Snarl—snapped at Frederick and nearly bit off his tail.

The whole shebang went 'round and 'round like a circus act—Frederick and Ishbu dashing here and there, pursued by the two rat terriers, hot eyed and eager, chased by the cook brandishing the cleaver and swearing in Chinese.

A fish slid off the counter and skidded across the floor, leaving a slimy trail of scales. Frederick deftly jumped over the fish, and Ishbu stumbled over it, but the dogs stopped for a second to sniff it until the cook kicked them away. The moment's distraction was all Frederick needed. With a powerful thrust of his hind legs, he leaped into a trash can standing in the corner.

"In here, Ishbu!" he cried, reaching down. Somewhat less gracefully, Ishbu grabbed hold of Frederick's outstretched paws and scrambled up, too.

No one saw them except the dogs. They circled the can, whining and barking. The cook's helper wiped his hands on his white apron and lifted the trash can out of the dogs' reach. "You want me to take out the trash?" he asked, opening the back door.

"Get rid of it!" yelled the cook, waving the cleaver. "Out, out!"

The helper carried the trash can into the alley. The dogs whined angrily, cheated of their prey. "Stop that noise!" yelled the cook.

Frederick, buried in limp noodles, shrimp shells, and broken almond cookies, peered over the top of the can. He saw the boy kick the door closed—right in the terriers' faces. The dogs were inside; the rats were out!

The boy tipped the trash can into the large garbage bin. Out tumbled eggshells and tea leaves, white cardboard cartons and crab shells. Out tumbled wonton wrappers and half-eaten water chestnuts. Out tumbled Frederick, followed by Ishbu.

A garbage truck rolled up behind the Chinese restaurant and slammed on the brakes. Two men stepped out.

"Not again!" cried Ishbu. The rats jumped out of the bin and ran under the fence for cover. They hid until the truck rattled away. Then they crept out.

"Let's climb the fence, where we can take a look around and catch up." Frederick grabbed his brother's paw, hauling Ishbu up behind him. They perched like squirrels on the top rail.

Dusk was falling. All around them, the lights of Chinatown blinked on.

GUNG HAY FAT CHOY! HAPPY NEW YEAR!

THE NEON DRAGON ON THE ROOF of the restaurant flickered to life. Frederick and Ishbu bathed in its red glow.

"Freddy," Ishbu whispered urgently, "I have to tell you— the Big Cheese is after Natasha!"

"Natasha!" Frederick's eyes widened. "I was on my way to meet her at the Good Fortune Herb Shop. We'll—"

The kitchen door banged open, and the terriers slunk into the alley.

"Quick, before they see us," whispered Frederick. "Follow me."

The brothers tiptoed rapidly along the top of the fence to the end of the alley, where they stopped in amazement. From their perch, the rats beheld Chinatown.

Red banners spanned the streets between the

pagoda-roofed shops. Skinned carcasses of fowl dangled from the shop-front beams, and raw fish lay heaped on open tables. Mobs of people crowded the sidewalks, jostling around wooden crates mounded high with red, yellow, and green vegetables. Delicious smells floated in the air. Ishbu's mouth watered.

Frederick heard the rattle of drums close at hand. A cheer rose from the crowd. This was no ordinary night. It was Chinese New Year!

Floats lit up like birthday cakes glided down the center of the main street, followed by dancers dressed in red lion costumes, girls twirling fans, and squadrons of martial arts students. As the two rats watched the sights, they exchanged stories about all that had happened since yesterday. "And that's how I came to be tied up," said Ishbu, just as a fusillade of firecrackers exploded below them. Acrid smoke drifted up to the fence. Frederick sneezed. When he opened his eyes, he spotted the sign for the Good Fortune Herb Shop. But was it safe to go there? If the dogs were tailing them, they'd lead the Big Cheese straight to Natasha. Frederick glanced below, but it was too dark and busy to see much. He strained to hear. Was that a yip or only the squeal of an excited child?

"We'd better get out of here in case the dogs come back," he told Ishbu.

The rats jumped from the fence. Step-by-step, they snuck through the mob, threading in and out of people's legs. Ishbu found a juicy water chestnut on the sidewalk and stopped to nibble.

"No time," said Frederick, pulling him away.

The two rats melted deeper into the crowd. Someone stepped on Ishbu's tail, and he yelped. Frederick turned to check behind them once more —and only a few feet away, he saw the terriers!

"Run!" he shouted to Ishbu. But the dogs had seen them. They howled and gave chase.

The panicked rats snaked through the throngs of people, sprinting between a girl and boy taking pictures, darting under a stroller. They dashed in front of a cart filled with sweet bean cakes and splashed through a puddle of spilled tea.

The tenacious terriers were close on their tails, snipping and snarling. People swatted at the dogs irritably but didn't notice the rats running for their lives.

Pop! Crack! Snap! A shower of small firecrackers exploded right under Ishbu's nose. He reared in fright and bolted away. Frederick raced after him.

They ran into the midst of the parade. Frederick's heart pounded so hard, he thought it would explode like one of the tiny red firecrackers.

They scooted under floats and whisked between marchers. The terriers charged after them, dogging their every move.

Ishbu's fur was slick and matted with sweat. His pink tongue hung out of his mouth. "I can't make it, Freddy!"

"Don't stop!" Frederick urged.

Frederick's eyes darted from side to side, searching for an escape route. But he saw nothing that would work.

A gigantic silk dragon swayed toward them, its head and rippling tail supported by a hundred dancers. *This might be our last chance*, thought Frederick.

He nudged Ishbu, and both rats hurled themselves beneath the spangled fabric, weaving in and out of the dancers' feet. Frederick hoped the dancers would be packed too closely for the dogs to follow, and for a while it looked as if the plan had worked, but then he heard the dogs give a triumphant bark.

There has to be some way to lose them. Frederick remembered a folktale Miss Dove had read in which a fox ran through a stream to throw a pack of hounds off his scent. But where could Frederick find a stream in the middle of a city street?

Frederick grabbed his brother and boosted him to the top of one of the dancer's black shoes. He hopped lightly on top of the man's other shoe, holding onto the pant leg to keep balance. Fortunately, the dancer was too busy—or too tired—to notice his hitchhikers.

Riding on top of the shoes, the rats left no scent to mark their trail. As the dragon pranced down the street, Frederick peeked out from under the silk fabric. Far behind them, he saw Snip and Snarl snuffling the pavement and looking bewildered.

The rats had lost their pursuers. For now.

GOOD FORTUNE HERB SHOP

FREDERICK AND ISHBU HOPPED OFF THEIR accommodating (but unsuspecting) transportation as the dragon danced past the Good Fortune Herb Shop. Hooking a ride on the dancers' feet had given the rats a chance to rest. They crouched outside the shop, sniffing for danger. No doggy odor fouled the air.

"Quick! In here!" A pointed, whiskery face with two bright eyes peered from a hole in the shop wall. With a last glance over his shoulder, Frederick shoved Ishbu inside and squeezed in after him.

The shop was closed for the night. Heavy shutters on the windows kept out the light and noise from the street. Frederick inhaled, and strange scents filled his nose. Ancient, dusty smells; weedy, herby smells; dry, powdery smells—foreign, exotic, tantalizing smells. And that familiar cinnamon fragrance . . . !

Frederick and Natasha rubbed noses. "I am so glad

you are here at last!" she said, squeezing Frederick's paw. "I am being so worried!" Then Natasha noticed Ishbu. "And Ishbu! What a surprise!"

Ishbu avoided her eyes. It was her fault they were in this mess.

"We were almost rat sushi for two terriers," said Frederick. "But I think we lost them in the crowd. At least, I hope so." He started to tell Natasha what they'd learned, but Ishbu interrupted.

"What is this place?" he asked, looking around.

"Good Fortune Herb Shop, owned by Mr. Yau Fong. He sells Chinese medicines," Natasha told them.

Frederick studied the shelves stacked with bottles and boxes, all decorated with brush calligraphy in red, gold, and black. Big glass jars held weird shrunken objects. Underneath Chinese characters were labels written in English: dried scallops, mummified scorpions, flattened lizards. He turned to Natasha and realized there was a smaller rodent standing next to her, the one who had led them into the shop.

"Mo-Mo, allow me to introduce my friends," Natasha said. "Frederick and his brother, Ishbu."

The mouse bowed slightly. "Colonel Morris Reginald Morris of Sowerby Bridge, England," he said. "At your service. Delighted, old chaps, simply delighted." His whiskers curled like a mustache, showing slightly protuberant front teeth. He had pink, rounded ears and a tail that tapered to a fine point. His thick fur was an unusual golden color, like champagne. Altogether, he was clearly too sleek to be a wild mouse. "Call me Mo-Mo," he added.

Ishbu sniffed him curiously. "Are you a pet mouse?" he asked.

"A pet mouse!" squeaked Mo-Mo in horror. "No, indeed! I'm a fancy mouse, bred for show—a thoroughbred, a grand champion. Why, I was Best-in-Show two years running at the London Meet!" He narrowed his eyes. "You are *sure* you haven't heard of me?"

Ishbu shrugged. "Afraid not."

"Pity," said Mo-Mo.

"How does a British show mouse end up in a Chinese herb shop in San Francisco?" Frederick asked.

"My owner is Mr. Wah Chun Fong," Mo-Mo explained with a smile. "His uncle, the proprietor of this shop, sent him to college in England, where he became a member of the Mouse Fanciers Club. It's a thrilling life. Mr. Fong and I travel the world, from competition to competition. Here today, there tomorrow! A bit like being a rock star, I imagine."

What a swell life that must be, thought Frederick enviously.

Brushing his ears, Mo-Mo went on. "We've been in San Francisco for the U.S. Cup. The competition was quite fierce—mice of every color: champagnes, silvers, blues, even a few lilacs like yourselves." He nodded at Frederick and Natasha. "But in the end, I took home the trophy." He groomed his whiskers modestly. "Tomorrow morning we fly to Geneva for the European Invitational, the highlight of the mouse show circuit."

"Gosh," said Ishbu. "A fancy mouse. Fancy that." He giggled at his own joke.

But Frederick had more pressing things on his mind. He turned to Natasha. "Tash," he whispered, "can we talk in private?"

CHAMPAGNE
AND CAVIAR

"OH, FREDERICK! NOT TO WORRY ABOUT darlink Mo-Mo," Natasha said. "I have been knowing him for ages. I never tell you, but once I am being on the rat show circuit myself." She fluttered her eyelashes at Mo-Mo, and Frederick felt a pang of jealousy.

"Okay, then," Frederick said uncertainly. He didn't quite trust the little mouse, but he didn't want to offend Natasha. "We have to warn you." Frederick took Natasha's paw in his. "The Big Cheese is after you!"

"Me? But what can he be wanting with me? How do you know this?"

Frederick described what had happened since Natasha left him at the burrow. Ishbu added his part of the tale. When the brothers finished, the three rats sat in silence for a moment, puzzling over this new information. Only Mo-Mo appeared uninterested.

He perched nearby on top of a spice cabinet, grooming.

"Big Cheese," Natasha murmured, her whiskers trembling. "It must be about . . . my father?"

"I don't know this Big Cheese chap," said Mo-Mo, slicking back his whiskers. "But he sounds a thoroughly nasty sort."

"He is," said Frederick curtly. He turned back to Natasha. "Don't worry, Tash. We'll get to the bottom of this. Did you find Dr. Liu?"

"Yes, but he is not knowing where my father has gone. Frederick, Dr. Liu did not write note!"

Frederick began to pace. "The Big Cheese wants your father for some reason. I'll bet *he* wrote the note to lure the professor to the restaurant. And now he wants you. . . . Did Dr. Liu tell you anything useful at all? Does he know what your father was working on?"

Natasha shook her head. "Is top secret. My father tells no one, not even his good friend. But Dr. Liu said it was some kind of formula. He believes it has something to do with dogs and cats."

Frederick shuddered. Dogs and cats were among a rat's greatest enemies. Only once had he known a cat that could be trusted. And never a dog. The professor must be a brave rat indeed to study those beasts!

"Did you say dogs and cats?" Ishbu scratched behind his ears. "That reminds me! There was this

strange story that I thought you'd like, Freddy. . . ."
He quickly filled them in on the newspaper article
he'd heard in Miss Dove's class.

Frederick looked thoughtful. "Could there be
some connection?"

"It said something about pet food, too," Ishbu
added. Just mentioning pet food made him hungry.
It had been a long time since his snack on the garbage
truck. His tummy growled loudly.

Mo-Mo laughed. "You must be famished, old
chaps. How about a spot of tea?"

Ishbu nodded eagerly. "And maybe a spot of food,
too?"

"Won't be a moment," said the mouse, and he
slipped down the stairs at the rear of the shop.

A short while later, Mo-Mo scampered back with
a fully laden tea tray. "Just a tidbit," he said. "Tuck in!"

The tray was heaped with goodies: egg rolls,
dumplings, prawns, bean sprouts, fragrant tea in a
china pot, and a fortune cookie for each of them.

In spite of their troubles—or maybe to distract
themselves—the meal was a lively one. Ishbu ate
heartily while Natasha and Mo-Mo reminisced about
their days together on the international show circuit.

Frederick picked at his food. Envy made the
savory morsels taste as appetizing as dirt. Natasha
looked prettier than ever. She seemed to sparkle as
she laughed with Mo-Mo. Natasha had led such a

glamorous life. *She's out of my league*, he thought miserably. *She's champagne and caviar, and I'm root beer and carrot sticks.*

Mo-Mo finally broke off his chatter. "I heard something of interest as I was downstairs getting tea." He looked at Natasha with concern. "I didn't want to tell you before," he said, "because I didn't want to spoil your meal. You look too thin, my dear. You mustn't let your worries make you ill."

Frederick rolled his eyes. He didn't believe the pompous little mouse could possibly know anything interesting.

Mo-Mo continued, "You might know that many of the shops in Chinatown are connected through their basements. But I'll wager you didn't know that the Good Fortune Herb Shop is connected to that place you were telling us about—the Red Dragon restaurant!"

Frederick sat up straight now, his whiskers as tense as wires. He hadn't realized. They were too close for comfort. Too close for Natasha's safety! He had to get her away as soon as possible. "Go on," he urged. "What did you hear?"

By now, even Ishbu was listening, and Natasha looked quite anxious. Mo-Mo appeared to enjoy the attention. He preened as he talked. "I must say, it took immense courage on my part. I crept through a mouse hole that I happen to know of into the basement next door to eavesdrop for you. Only a brave mouse such as myself would have taken such a risk." He took a moment to smooth his golden fur.

Frederick was ready to take the mouse by the scruff of his golden neck and shake him like a dog shakes a bone. "And. You. Heard. What?" He forced the question out through gritted teeth.

"I heard those dogs you spoke of . . . Snip, did you say? And Snarl? Talking about that big fellow. The evil chap. I remember now—the Big Cheese. They spoke of your father, my dear." He leaned toward Natasha. "You must be brave, too," he told her, patting her paw.

"Go on!" ordered Frederick. "What did they say about the professor?"

"The Big Cheese has gone to Scotland. And"— the mouse paused for a dramatic flourish—"he's taken the professor with him!"

YE TAKE
THE HIGH ROAD

"SCOTLAND!" CRIED NATASHA.

"Scotland!" echoed Ishbu, wrinkling his nose. "Where's that?"

Frederick felt as flat as a popped balloon. "North of England. Across the Atlantic Ocean. Half a world from here."

"Across the world! Freddy, how will we ever get there?" Ishbu began to suck on his tail.

"By blimp? Submarine? Hot-air balloon like our last journey? I don't know how to get there, Ishbu." Frederick shook his head.

"There must be some way," said Natasha. "I must be saving my father!"

Mo-Mo gave a delicate cough. "I might be of some assistance in this matter," he said. "As I mentioned, my owner and I fly to Geneva tomorrow. We refuel in Inverness, in the north of Scotland. Allow me to drop you on the way."

"Thank you, dear friend," said Natasha. She hugged the mouse.

Frederick watched them unhappily. "I guess you won't need me anymore, then," he told Natasha. "Mo-Mo can take care of you."

"That's right," said Ishbu with relief. "We'll go on home." He grinned at Frederick, but his brother didn't respond. "Isn't that right, Freddy? Home? Miss Dove's class? Our snug cage?"

Frederick didn't look at him. His eyes were on Natasha.

"Please come," Natasha pleaded softly, holding out both paws. "I need you to be helping rescue my father in Scotland. What would I be doing without you?"

Frederick paused a second, then took her paws. "Of course we'll come!" he said. "You can count on us!"

Ishbu looked horrified. "Fly? In a plane? Oh, no, Freddy. I can't. You know I get airsick." He looked a bit green around the whiskers just at the thought. Then he sighed. "Okay, if you go, I go." There was no way he was going to be left behind *this* time!

"But won't your owner notice us stowing away?" Natasha asked.

"I'll hide you in my cage," Mo-Mo said. "*Mine* is the Rolls-Royce of cages—luxurious, roomy. I could easily accommodate a pack of rats. Lots of comfortable

—and concealing—bedding. Leave it to me, old chaps. Leave it to me."

∞

The rats spent the rest of the night sleeping (Ishbu and Natasha) and pacing (Frederick) in a hole behind the spice cabinet of the herb shop. In the morning, before the shop opened, Mo-Mo hid them on the lower level of his four-story cage, carefully mounding shavings over them until they were buried deep in fluffy bedding.

Mo-Mo's owner, a nearsighted young man in spectacles, never noticed the stowaways as he snapped up the sides of the cage and loaded it into the limo waiting outside.

Ishbu began to feel carsick right away and poked his nose out of the cage for some fresh air, risking detection. But they made it safely to the airfield. From there, it was but a matter of minutes until they boarded Mr. Fong's aeroplane.

"A private aeroplane?" asked Frederick, unable to hide his awe.

"Oh, didn't I tell you?" trilled Mo-Mo. "We always travel this way."

The interior of the plane was elegant, with eight spacious leather seats. Mr. Fong strapped the cage into a seat next to a window.

"He wants me to have plenty of light," Mo-Mo told the rats. "So good for the coat. You chaps ought to try it." He licked his paw and sleeked his whiskers. His champagne fur sparkled like—well, champagne —in the sunlight.

A pint-size kitchen and several closets were located in the rear of the plane. Frederick figured the closets were for luggage, and indeed, as he peeked out of the bedding, Mr. Fong opened one and stowed his suitcase inside. Then Mr. Fong went to the cockpit to talk with the pilot, leaving Mo-Mo and the rats alone in the cabin. The rats shook off the shavings and looked out of the cage.

There was an unfamiliar smell. Ishbu sneezed. "Bay Rum," Mo-Mo informed them. "Mr. Fong's favorite cologne."

The outside doors closed with a bang, and the plane rattled as the engines roared to life.

FROM SEA TO SHINING SEA

 FREDERICK GLANCED ACROSS THE cage at Natasha. She'd lost the radiance she'd had yesterday. He told her, "It won't be long now. I'm sure we can rescue your father."

"So hard to be knowing where to search when we get to Scotland," she said, shaking her head.

Hoping to cheer her up, Frederick softly began to recite one of his favorite poems: "My heart's in the Highlands . . ."

To his surprise, Natasha spoke the next line, "My heart is not here."

Their eyes met. They said the next line together: "My heart's in the Highlands a-chasing the deer."

"You like Robert Burns, too?" Frederick asked.

She smiled. "My favorite poet."

The plane took off, and soon they were soaring above San Francisco. Mr. Fong settled down in his seat across the aisle with a Chinese-language news-paper. When they were sure Mr. Fong was engrossed in his paper, Frederick and Natasha climbed to the top floor of the cage. Frederick pressed his nose to the bars and squinted out the window.

How he longed for a telescope or even a pair of binoculars! But the view was still stirring. He spotted the slender white column of Coit Tower, the famous San Francisco landmark, the orange span of the Golden Gate Bridge, and the sparkling waters of San Francisco Bay with the island of Alcatraz floating in the middle like a pirate ship. The plane banked and climbed above the clouds. Frederick bruxed contentedly, holding Natasha's paw.

They soared across the United States, Frederick searching every break in the clouds for a glimpse of some landform he'd heard Miss Dove describe—the white-capped ridges of the Sierra Nevada; the Great Salt Lake, shining like a mirror; the bare and lonely plain of the Great Basin; the towering majesty of the Rockies.

"Amber waves of grain," Frederick murmured to Natasha. "Purple mountain majesties." He couldn't help but feel excited. For here he was—on another daring adventure! Off to see the world!

From time to time, Mr. Fong checked on his prize-winning mouse, and—while the rats hid beneath the bedding—replenished Mo-Mo's food and water.

The shadow of the plane looked tiny as it traced

its way across the prairies and cornfields of the Midwest. The sky darkened, and soon nothing more could be seen but the glimmer of lights from towns and cities far below. Frederick yawned. His eyes, heavy with sleep, closed. He didn't even wake up when they stopped to re-fuel.

He had woken only once during the trip across the Atlantic, looking out in time to see the glittering metropolis of New York City falling away behind them, the Statue of Liberty as tiny as a doll; and then nothing but the moonlight on the waves of the Atlantic Ocean.

Beside him, Natasha was curled up, her nose tucked under her tail, fast asleep. Frederick gazed at her tenderly and closed his eyes.

And what were Mo-Mo and Ishbu doing all this time? Ishbu helped himself to some of the superb, first-rate snacks—high-protein mouse pellets and organic kibble—that Mo-Mo's owner had so thoughtfully provided. While Ishbu munched and gnawed, snacked and smacked, Mo-Mo kindly entertained him with tales of all the competitions he'd ever entered.

All of them. Every last one. His stories went on for hours. And every single one of them started exactly the same: "Have I ever told you, old chap, about the time I . . ." They all sounded the same in the middle, too: "But of course, no one could compete with *my* coat (or ears, eyes, tail, carriage, gait, charm, et cetera, et cetera . . .)." They even all ended the same: "And that's how I won (topped, aced, captured the prize, triumphed, and so on and so forth)."

In short, Mo-Mo was a B.O.R.E. (a Bushel of Repetitions Everlasting)! But Ishbu didn't really mind. Much. Mo-Mo's chatter made a soothing noise to accompany his naps and nibbling.

After midnight, Ishbu, who wasn't as airsick as he'd feared, looked out the window and saw the cold, white twinkle of stars above and the vast, black Atlantic Ocean below.

"Are we in heaven?" Ishbu wondered aloud. He yawned, sticking his tongue out, and went back to sleep.

And so the hours slid past. At last the faint streaks of dawn lit the window, and Frederick blinked. He broke his fast with some of Mo-Mo's mouse pellets and a good, long drink of water.

Ishbu and Natasha were still sound asleep. Frederick assumed the smaller lump under the shavings was Mo-Mo. *Probably shavings are good for the coat,* thought Frederick scornfully.

A change in the pitch of the engine's roar startled him. He climbed up to peer out the window and saw—

Green fields! Gray stone walls! Castle ruins! Church spires! Through the streaks of rain spitting against the window, Frederick caught his first glimpse of bonny Scotland.

I'LL TAKE
THE LOW ROAD

FREDERICK WATCHED EAGERLY AS the plane flew low over Scotland. Unlike Ishbu—who had cringed beneath the shavings, eyes squeezed tight, body quivering—Frederick had actually enjoyed the takeoff. The never-to-be missed moment when the aeroplane left the ground and "slipped the surly bonds of Earth"; the landing gear retracting with a groan; the excitement of knowing you are really on your way.

He anticipated the equally thrilling moment when the wheels touched down; the roar of the engine as the big machine braked; the tremble of the aircraft, once more earthbound; the feeling of a giant, unseen hand pressing you to your seat.

The plane hit a pocket of turbulence and bounced, jarring open one of the closets in the rear of the plane. Frederick might have missed it, but he had just turned around to wink comfortingly at Natasha, who was waking up, and the movement of the door caught his eye.

Mo-Mo wasn't in the cage. He was in the closet, and he didn't see Frederick watching as he spoke to someone who was in the closet with him. A hairy snout poked out just a fraction of an inch.

It was enough for Frederick to see who Mo-Mo was talking to. His bones turned to ice. Snarl!

He scrambled next to Natasha and nipped Ishbu on the tail to wake him.

"Wha—?" said Ishbu sleepily.

Frederick hissed, "Snarl is on board. Maybe Snip as well. They're in cahoots with Mo-Mo. Mo-Mo must have used Mr. Fong's cologne to hide their scent. He's betrayed us."

"No!" squeaked Natasha. "I am not believing it."

"See for yourself," said Frederick. "But quietly. We've got to make a plan."

Natasha climbed up to the second floor to see better and came back down, looking pale and shaky. "Is true. I see with my own eyes. What are we going to do?"

"They must be taking us to the Big Cheese," said Frederick.

They were trapped in a small plane, on the way to their worst enemy. To be delivered like a package. Frederick fought down his panic.

"We must escape," said Natasha. She seemed calmer now. Frederick gazed at her in admiration.

"Escape!" squeaked Ishbu. "How can we escape? We're in an aeroplane! Miles up in the sky!"

"Not so very high," said Frederick, thinking hard. "And the plane is going to land for refueling. We can sneak off then."

"It could be too late," argued Natasha. "They could be having hench-beasts meet the plane when we refuel. We must escape now."

"Stay here," said Frederick. "I'll go see where we are."

He slipped out of the cage and climbed on the top of the seat. The closet was shut now. Mr. Fong had gone up front to sit with the pilot. The cabin was empty. Frederick examined the windows. None of them would open, but there was an emergency exit across the aisle.

Frederick gazed out the nearest window. They were flying very low over a lake as brown as cold tea, cupped between green hills. Frederick knew that a Scottish lake was called a loch. He wondered if this might be Loch Ness—possibly the most famous loch in the world—home to the fabled sea serpent known as Nessie.

Natasha and Ishbu crawled up next to him. Natasha leaned over his shoulder to look out the window.

"We must jump here," she said, her voice shaky but determined, "and we must go now. Better to take our chances than be taken by Big Cheese!"

"Do you still have your nail file?" asked Frederick.

Natasha's eyes gleamed as she showed it to him. She darted across the aisle to the emergency exit. "I open, yes?" she said, and when Frederick nodded, she began to work the lock with the thin silver file.

It took all three rats to pull open the door, and even then it opened only a few inches. The rush of air was tremendous.

"Jump on the count of three!" shouted Frederick, his whiskers blowing in the wind.

It all happened so fast. Before the rats could jump, Snip grabbed Natasha from behind and yanked her away from the door.

Frederick felt a hard shove on his back, and the next thing he knew, he was sucked out of the aircraft. He fell, whirling like a leaf caught in a hurricane. Beside him, he saw Ishbu tumbling nose over tail. Side by side they hurled through the air, twisting as they dropped.

"Ta, ta, old chaps," Mo-Mo called from the plane door as the brothers plunged toward the water. "Happy landings!"

The aeroplane roared away.

Part Two:
UNDERGROUND

Three may keep a secret, if two of them are dead.
—Ben Franklin

Me and my true love will never meet again . . .
—"Loch Lomond" Traditional

FREE FALL

SEEN FROM A SATELLITE ORBITING Earth, Loch Ness looks like a long serpent bisecting the Highlands of Scotland. Closer to the ground—from a plane, for instance—Loch Ness looks like a brown seal, basking between the heathery hills. From a boat on the water, Loch Ness is as narrow as a misty, fog-bound river. But from the point of view of a creature sitting at the water's edge, Loch Ness is as enormous as an ocean, crowned with white-capped waves stretching from shore to distant shore.

If only the brothers had thought to wear parachutes or life vests! But who could have guessed Mo-Mo's duplicity? Not Ishbu. Not Frederick, even with his suspicions.

Without parachutes, they plummeted like sky-divers in free fall. Ishbu scrabbled at the air with all four paws as if trying to find a toehold. But there was nothing—nothing but air and space between the falling rats and the hard, cold waters of Loch Ness.

They spun and twisted—first tail down, then snout down, paws akimbo. The surface of the loch came closer and closer. When Frederick finally fell into the lake, there was barely a splash to disturb the ancient waters. The darkness closed over his head.

Suddenly entering frigid water causes a great shock to the body. Systems shut down. Breathing stops momentarily as the diaphragm contracts, forcing air out of the lungs with a *whoosh*. The heart slows, or —in extreme cases—might even stop.

Frederick's heart didn't stop. Not quite. But everything went black. He never heard Ishbu's faint splash seconds after his own.

Neither rat saw the lone figure crouched beneath the ruins of Urquhart Castle on the bonny, bonny bank of Loch Ness.

But it saw them.

Stillness surrounded Frederick when he opened his eyes. He blinked. Nothing but darkness as thick as velvet. He used his nose: the damp, musty smell of earth. To a human, the smell would have raised goose bumps—thoughts of unsealed tombs, rotting bones, the dank smell of the grave. But to a rodent, the smell spoke of underground burrows, safe havens—home. The dark was as comforting to

Frederick as a favorite quilt.

Frederick listened, and a faint snoring, as familiar as his own breathing, reached his ears. Ishbu! Ishbu was alive!

Frederick tried to roll over to snuffle Ishbu's fur, to nuzzle his neck, but a fearful ache in all his joints prevented him from moving. His head throbbed. He lay still once more and, shutting his eyes, he slept.

The next time Frederick woke, he couldn't see, but the aroma of food—pungent and savory—wafted to his nostrils. Despite his aching body, he managed to crawl toward the smell. Food! Water! Where had they come from?

Frederick found Ishbu by following the sound of his snoring. "Wake up," he called, nudging his brother. "Food!" But Ishbu snored on.

What's wrong with him? Frederick wondered. He'd never seen Ishbu sleep through a meal before. Why didn't he wake?

Out of the dark came a low growl, as if answering his thoughts. "He's in a coma."

Frederick gasped.

He heard the scrape of flint on stone, and a wavering light filled the burrow as someone, or something, lit a lantern. The glow illuminated a broad, striped face; wide paws; wary eyes.

A male badger, a boar! Although he'd never seen one in the flesh, Frederick recognized the creature immediately from Miss Dove's animal books. A shiver ran through him. Badgers were omnivorous. This meant they ate everything: grubs, earthworms, roots and tubers—and rats!

The creature drew himself up, nearly filling the small chamber with his bulk. His eyes glowed green in the lantern light. His claws were long and slightly curved, each one a tool—or a weapon. He drew back his black lips, and Frederick could see his ivory teeth.

"'Twas a wicked fall you laddies took," said the badger. "The wee beastie is unconscious. He may wake anytime. He may sleep for weeks. None can say." The badger shook his head. "He may die."

Tears sprang to Frederick's eyes. Die! Not Ishbu!

ISHBU SLEEPS

ISHBU LAY ON HIS BACK, NOSE raised, eyes closed, and mouth open. His pink paws were curled by his sides, his tail stretched out beneath him. Frederick watched his brother's chest rise and fall, rise and fall, with every breath.

Frederick knew that a coma was a kind of deep sleep, a blackout, a complete loss of consciousness sometimes caused by a head injury. Ishbu must have been knocked out when he hit the water. That the rats survived at all was no doubt due to the badger.

"Thank you for rescuing us," Frederick told him. But the badger shook his shaggy head.

"Not I," said the badger. "Ye owe that to Mrs. McLeod, the hedgehog who lives by the loch. Bit of a busybody, she is, but a kindhearted soul. Whilst she was out foraging, she saw ye fall into the loch. She pulled ye out and brought ye here, to my sett. All strangers to the glen must be inspected by me, Dooncan MacTavish." (Frederick noticed that he pronounced *Duncan* in the Scottish fashion.) The badger went on. "'Tis the custom. I am the laird o' the glen."

Frederick wanted to question him further, but the old boar trundled into a tunnel, leaving the lantern, food, and water behind.

Frederick slapped Ishbu's face, rubbed his paws, and sprinkled water over him. "Ishbu!" he cried. "Wake up! It's me, Freddy!" His efforts were fruitless. Ishbu snored peacefully, showing his tiny teeth and pink tongue. Frederick threw himself down beside his brother, dropping his head into his paws in despair.

This was all his fault! He should have insisted that Ishbu stay safely at home. Now everything was ruined. Natasha and her father in the clutches of the Big Cheese. Ishbu in a sleep so deep he might never recover. And the two of them, helpless and alone, in the burrow of an omnivorous Scottish badger!

∞

Day and night had no meaning in this subterranean world. Frederick slept and woke and ate and drank. Gradually, his sprains and aches became less painful; his bruises changed to purple, then yellow, and then faded away. But Ishbu showed no signs of waking.

Every so often, Frederick spooned hot broth or dribbled cool water down Ishbu's throat, just enough to keep him alive. Ishbu swallowed but made no other response.

Omnivorous or not, the badger seemed in no hurry to eat the two rats. Frederick wondered if he was fattening them up for later. Every day Duncan brought oatcakes and bowls of porridge or broth. Occasionally he added a side dish of chewy earthworms for protein. Simple, hearty foods suitable for invalids.

Several times Duncan changed their bedding, exchanging it for a fresh pile of thick, springy heather. He rarely spoke but stood with his paws folded across his great belly, an unreadable expression on his striped face as he watched Frederick care for his brother.

In spite of the boar's kind treatment, Frederick didn't trust him. Why did Duncan let them stay? Frederick nibbled his toenails restlessly. If only they could leave, escape, flee! He yearned to be off searching for Natasha. But with Ishbu unconscious, what could he do?

Gradually, Frederick realized the badger left the den every night (he assumed it was night, as badgers are nocturnal, like rats). More than once, Frederick was awakened by strange knocks and muttered words. Animals came and went on quiet paws. *What errands in the dead of night are these? What dastardly deeds, what midnight excursions are afoot?*

Frederick had to get Ishbu out of here—carry him,

drag him, whatever it took. He'd find somewhere out of harm's way, somewhere hidden, somewhere far from predators, hench-beasts, and traitors. They mustn't sit here like ducks being fattened for a feast!

So the next night, after Frederick heard the badger leave, he left Ishbu behind on his bed of heather and slipped out of the chamber.

Nose twitching, he explored a passage leading off the main tunnel. There must be an exit hole. The main entrance was out of the question. For all he knew, the badger stood guard every night, waiting for them to emerge. It would have to be the back entrance.

And there *must* be a back entrance. Frederick knew instinctively that every den or burrow needed an escape route—a tunnel or exit that a creature could use to flee to safety if a snake or weasel crawled into the burrow.

The tunnels of the badger's sett seemed to run for miles, branching off into small rooms here and there. Most rooms were empty, mere cells hollowed out of the dirt or filled with winter stores—piles of roots and tubers, dried onions and herbs, shocks of oats. But in one vacant chamber, Frederick caught a different scent: mothballs and old fabric. His curiosity was piqued by the odd combination. He followed the smell to an alcove. Propped up against the earthen wall was a pole wrapped in fabric. Frederick lifted it, and a silk flag unfurled in a swath of red. He smoothed it out. The flag was worn in spots, nearly threadbare. *How many years has it been hidden?*

Frederick swept his paw across the fabric. A faded design in blue, green, black, and yellow was emblazoned across the front.

His whiskers pricked. A crest? A shield? A coat of arms? He blew on the fabric gently to get the dust off and saw a world map bordered by letters. The script was old-fashioned and hard to read. Frederick traced the embroidery with one paw tip as he spelled out the letters.

A.B.O.B.

He'd seen that design before!

ISHBU WAKES

FREDERICK REPLACED THE FLAG and continued searching the sett but found nothing. If there was an exit hole (and he was still convinced there was), it was well hidden. Disappointed, he went back to the chamber and curled up on the heather next to Ishbu.

Frederick's sleep was restless and punctuated with nightmares. He dreamed he was back at Wilberforce Harrison Elementary School running laps on the wheel in his cage. Miss Dove was there, wearing a sweet-smelling corsage of violets. Frederick's nose twitched in his sleep. Miss Dove offered him a carrot stick, and he reached for it, but just as he was about to take a bite, she vanished, replaced by a golden dragon. Frederick tried to run, but his legs wouldn't move. The dragon reared up, its teeth as enormous as tusks. Frederick whimpered but didn't wake. The dream changed again, and now the dragon had Snarl's face. The terrier raised his muzzle and howled.

"Freddy?"

The dog sounded just like Ishbu. Frederick stirred.

"Freddy?"

It wasn't a dream. Someone was shaking him. Frederick rolled over and rubbed the sleep out of his eyes. Ishbu sat next to him. Ishbu was awake! Frederick sat up and sniffed Ishbu's fur. He smelled healthy. No trace of illness.

"Where are we?" Ishbu asked. "What's going on? Is there anything to eat? I'm so empty my tummy echoes."

Frederick laughed, his whiskers curling up. Good old Ishbu! Always the same!

Frederick led the way to one of the storerooms he'd investigated earlier. They munched on pungent white roots—crisp, chewy, and rather like radishes —while Frederick filled Ishbu in on the days he'd spent in a coma and the mysterious badger who'd sheltered them.

When they'd finished eating, Ishbu sat back on his haunches and cleaned his whiskers. "What now?" he asked.

Frederick sighed. "I don't know. The dogs and Mo-Mo have Natasha. I'm sure they took her to the Big Cheese."

"Mo-Mo works for the Big Cheese, huh?" said Ishbu.

"He must," said Frederick. "I'll bet he got orders from Snip and Snarl when he went downstairs to get tea. All that talk about his brave eavesdropping, hah! But we don't know where they are or why the Big Cheese wants Natasha and her father. Think, Ishbu! When you were in his lair, did he say anything—anything at all—that would give us a hint?"

Ishbu rubbed his ears in thought and shook his head. "Nope. Sorry, Freddy."

Frederick strode up and down the storeroom, his tail dragging in the dust. "We have to get above-ground, figure out where we are—and somehow, we've got to rescue Natasha and the professor! But first," he said, taking Ishbu by the paw, "now that you've eaten, let me show you something odd."

He led Ishbu to the room with the flag. After examining it, Ishbu turned to Frederick and shrugged. "So? I don't get it. What's so important about this?"

Frederick pointed. "Look closer. Don't you recognize it? It's the same design as the one on Professor Ratinsky's medal. The medal that was stolen from his burrow!"

Ishbu laughed. "But Freddy, you forget—I was never in Professor Ratinsky's burrow."

"Ah, of course! You'll have to trust me. It's the exact design." Frederick rubbed his muzzle. "But what's the connection?"

"Coincidence?" Ishbu suggested.

"I don't trust coincidences," said Frederick gloomily. "There's danger here, Ishbu. I can feel it."

At that moment, a sound in the tunnel caught Frederick's attention. A series of thumps like—paw steps. The badger!

THE GUILTY FLEE
WHERE NONE PURSUE

 "Quick!" said Frederick. "He's coming!"

Ishbu looked puzzled. "I don't hear anything, Freddy."

Frederick glanced at the ancient flag with its baffling inscription. He didn't want to be found rummaging through the badger's things like a common pack rat. "Come on, Ishbu! This way!"

The brothers loped down the tunnel. Frederick led the way, his eyes straining to see in the dark. Ishbu ran behind, sniffing for danger. The tunnel twisted and turned, branching off in new directions. It was impossible to know which turn to take. Whenever the rats reached a fork, they froze, undecided. Then Frederick would gallop ahead, Ishbu following close on his tail.

Several times the rats were trapped by a passage that simply dead ended. They'd double back, take another fork, and race on, always with their noses raised, searching for the clean scent of fresh air, the scent that might lead them to an exit. But the air in the tunnel stayed earthy, musty, and stale.

Behind them, as steady and measured as a pulse, came the lumbering thud of paw steps. No matter where they ran, no matter which way they went, the heavy scrape of claws followed. Never gaining on them, but never out of range, either.

Panting, Ishbu rested against a dirt wall. "I'm all done in," he gasped. Frederick realized, with a pang, that this rat race was simply too much to ask of his brother. Frederick pressed against Ishbu, supporting and comforting him.

With a cascade of dirt, the earthen wall crumbled away, and the rat brothers toppled through—into a hidden den.

They lay in a tangled heap on the floor. Stunned, the rats could hardly take in the scene. Five angry badgers gathered around Duncan, the old boar. Mutters gave way to badger sounds: chirrs and shouts, barks and snarls, high-pitched keckers. Fists pounded; feet stamped. Duncan ignored the ruckus, as calm as the eye of a whirlwind. None of the badgers had noticed the rats—yet.

"Dooncan MacTavish," a russet badger shouted, shaking his fist under the boar's nose, "will ye no listen? Ye are a traitor to the clan! Giving aid to the enemy! Those rats are a danger to us and oor plans. I say fling them into the loch with the monster afore they betray us!"

"Hush yoor blether, Angus!" said a badger with a wicked-looking grin. "Waste o' good food. Munch them up for supper, says I."

The noise stopped abruptly as a seventh badger pushed his pointed muzzle through the new hole in the wall. "I found these two sneaking around the sett," he growled, pointing to the dazed rats.

Six pairs of eyes stared at the intruders. Six jaws opened wide. Only Duncan sat without moving.

"Spies!" shouted a dark-haired badger. The six badgers advanced.

Frederick and Ishbu huddled together, completely surrounded. What had they stumbled into? A den meeting of the badger clan? The European branch of the Bilgewater Brigade? Menacing badgers intent on mayhem, violence, and possibly supper?

Frederick, aware of how puny he was compared to these burly beasts, scrambled to his feet and stood protectively over Ishbu. Ishbu still cowered on the floor, sucking his tail. Frederick clenched his paws. Undeterred by the odds, he would fight—to the death, if need be! He hissed and bared his teeth, trying his best to look brave, but his insides jiggled like jelly.

"Kill them!" shouted the russet badger named

Angus. "Afore they can betray us!"

"Aye," growled the others.

"Wait!" shouted a badger with broad stripes on his face. "We'd best find oot whit they know. They may be working for *him*." He spat.

"Aye, MacDuff," said a brawny badger. "Tie them up. Beat the truth oot o' them!"

In moments, the badgers had tied Frederick and Ishbu tail to tail. The brawny badger stood over them; the rest gathered close. The smell of musk was overpowering.

Frederick spotted Duncan behind the others, his eyes half closed. Why didn't he speak up? He didn't even look interested. Did he want them killed, too? Then why had he fed and sheltered them?

The brawny badger growled deep in his throat. "A'right laddies," he said. "Ye'll no escape."

"Tell us whit ye know!" barked Angus. The others growled in agreement.

"Nothing!" blurted Ishbu. "We don't know anything! We aren't working for anybody. We came to rescue Natasha—"

"Stop, Ishbu!" cried Fredrick. But Ishbu couldn't be stopped.

"—and Professor Ratinsky!"

The professor's name had an astonishing effect. The den became as quiet as if Ishbu had uttered a magic charm. Six badgers stared at the rats and then rapidly left the den, melting away one by one into the darkness of the tunnel.

Frederick and Ishbu were alone in the burrow with Duncan.

THE HEART OF
A BADGER

FREDERICK STARED INTO DUNCAN'S EYES.

"Coom wi' me," growled the big badger. He untied them.

Frederick felt Ishbu trembling beside him as the badger led them through a passage. Where was he taking them? Frederick tried to be brave. He searched his heart—but found only fear. He had tried to trust Mo-Mo, and look where it got them! As they padded through the tunnel, he kept his eye out for possible escape routes. He saw none.

The badger squeezed through a narrow opening. Frederick and Ishbu followed and found themselves in a pleasant, well-lighted room.

"Join me in a wee spot of tea, laddies?"

Frederick nodded. Duncan wasn't growling after all, Frederick realized. It was only his thick Scottish burr. Frederick's mouth hung slightly open as he gazed around the room. This was no earthy chamber scraped out of the underground!

The light came from a peat fire burning in a fireplace. Three comfortable armchairs were pulled up before the fire. Over the fireplace hung a shield with a crest of thistles crossed with heather. The mantel held a tin tea caddy with a picture of the queen of England, a china clock, and a tartan biscuit box. Frederick's mouth watered as the badger set out plump pieces of shortbread on a patterned plate.

The rest of the chamber was furnished simply. China platters and teacups were displayed in a tall cupboard. Four stools were set around a long wooden table. On the table were a toolbox and what appeared to be a stack of blueprints.

Duncan poured three cups of tea, and after handing one to each rat, he settled himself in a chair. He gestured to the brothers, and they climbed up into the other armchairs. Frederick eyed the badger warily, but Duncan seemed to mean them no harm. At least for now.

The boar swallowed his tea and set the cup and saucer down. He bent his great black-and-white- striped head toward the rats. "Well, laddies, I have a few questions afore I decide whither to eat ye noo or save ye for later." He winked, and Frederick's eyes widened before he realized Duncan was—in his own way—*teasing*.

The badger glared at the rats from beneath his bushy eyebrows (they looked like eyebrows to Frederick, anyway). "Who are ye? How came ye to be in the loch? Why were ye pokin' aboot my sett? And—most important—whit do ye know o' Professor Ratinsky?"

Frederick took a hesitant sip of his tea while he considered how much they ought to tell Duncan. *Could they trust him? Where did he go on his nighttime outings? What did they know of him, really, or any of these badgers?* He said nothing.

Ishbu, however, felt no reserve. As usual. He slurped his tea and munched his shortbread, turning it around and around in his paws to nibble all the sides. With crumbs sticking to his whiskers, he eagerly began to tell Duncan about their search to find the professor, encountering Mo-Mo and the Big Cheese, and being pushed out of the aeroplane. Frederick tried to stop him but then realized they had nothing to lose at this point. It was all over in a matter of minutes—their quest revealed.

Duncan smiled, and Frederick quailed at the sight of all those teeth. Frederick squinted and tried to look fierce, which is hard to do when you are a pet rat and your opponent is a wild badger.

"Now you know our story," Frederick said, hoping his voice didn't shake. "It's your turn. Who were those other badgers? Why did they call us spies?" He paused and surveyed the cozy room, gathering courage.

"And what," Frederick added, "does A.B.O.B. stand for?"

THE A.B.O.B.

THE BADGER FOLDED HIS FRONT PAWS. His forearms were heavily muscled and barred with sable stripes. His paws were the size of spades, and Frederick thought of those miles of underground tunnels and passageways that someone—Duncan?—had dug into the earth.

"Laddies," said the badger gruffly, "I dinnae know nothin' aboot A.B.O.B. Dinnae ask me again."

Frederick refused to be intimidated. "You can't bluff me," he said. "You know something. I saw how the others reacted when Ishbu said Professor Ratinsky's name. I saw the flag with the initials A.B.O.B. The same initials—the same design—as on Professor Ratinsky's medal!"

Duncan grunted. "Ye've seen the professor? Recently?" There was a note of anxiety in his voice that Frederick hadn't heard before.

Frederick shook his head. "No. But his daughter,

Natasha, showed me his photograph." He banged his empty teacup into the saucer. "Don't you understand?" he cried. "Professor Ratinsky and Natasha are in danger! Whatever you know that might help, tell us." He opened his paws and added, "Please."

The badger scratched his chin and sighed. "I see we've got to trust each other, laddies," he said. "But may curses rain down upon ye if ye breathe so much as a whisker of whit I'm aboot to tell ye t' anyone else!"

Ishbu took the last piece of shortbread on the plate and offered half to Frederick, who refused. Only Ishbu could eat at a time like this.

"A.B.O.B. stands for Ancient Brotherhood of Badgers," said Duncan. "We are a secret society formed long ago t' bring together the badger clans in a single cause—peaceful coexistence of humans and beasts." Duncan picked up the biscuit box.

"The Brotherhood has lodges all around the world —Britain, France, Germany, Switzerland, Russia, Japan—anywhere badgers live. The knowledge o' the Brotherhood is passed doon from badger t' badger, through the clans."

"A secret society!" repeated Ishbu. "With passwords, and paw shakes, and ceremonies, and stuff like that?" His eyes shone.

Duncan set down the biscuit box. Ishbu eyed it hopefully, but Duncan didn't notice and went on. "We know all aboot the Big Cheese and his gang. He has been a thorn in the side of oor Brotherhood for years. His goals are the opposite of oors. We want humans and beasts to live together; he wants all humans dead and himself as laird o' the beasts. We watch him carefully, tracking his moves and trying to thwart his plans. As for the professor? An admirable rat. The Brotherhood awarded him oor highest honor, the Benevolence Medal."

"That's the medal I saw," said Frederick. "In the photograph!"

"Aye," said Duncan. He started to say more but then stopped. He stared into the fire for a long time, stroking his whiskers. Finally, he leaned forward, his huge paws on the arms of his chair. His eyes bored into Frederick's. "Whit if I told ye," he whispered, "that we know quite well where to find the professor?"

BENEATH
THE CASTLE RUINS

FREDERICK LEAPED TO HIS PAWS. "And Natasha?"

Duncan didn't answer.

Frederick pestered the badger to tell them more, but Duncan refused. "I can say no more 'til ye've met the others," he said, heaving himself up. "Coom with me."

The rats followed him down the passage, and in a short time, they smelled something they hadn't smelled in days—fresh air! The animals scrambled up a tunnel and emerged into the night. Frederick sucked in fragrant breaths—cold and crisp as apple cider, with a hint of heather and the murky waters of Loch Ness. Above, billions of stars blazed in the inky sky, unpolluted by city lights. An owl hooted nearby and, feeling exposed, Frederick shuddered. He missed the cover of tall buildings and narrow alleyways or—even better—the shelter of his own cage.

"Oor meeting hall is over there," Duncan told them, "beneath the ruins o' Urquhart Castle."

The wind tousled Frederick's fur as they made their way up the slope to the ruined square tower on the edge of the loch. Frederick gazed up. The roof was long gone, and the windows as well, leaving only rectangular holes gaping in the stone like empty eye sockets. He could see the glimmer of stars through them.

Duncan paused next to a bare thorn tree. He parted the bushes under it with his paws, revealing a hole hidden in the bank. Frederick caught the scent of herbs. The muffled sound of bagpipes came from deep within the earth.

Duncan stopped them with his paw. "Ye'd best let me go in first. There may be a wee spot of bother aboot this." He went into the hole, then seemed to change his mind and stuck his head back out of the burrow.

"Jist a word, before ye coom in," he said. "They're brave lads, and loyal, but not used to rats. So pay no mind t' Angus-the-Russet, he's aye crabbit; and Niall may be brash and hot-tempered, but he's a bonny fighter if your back's t' the wall. There's Brock, he's a'right, jist a bit of a jokester; and bold MacDuff is the boar to have beside ye in a battle. Then there's steady Sandy—ye'll know him by his tawny coat—and old Ramsey, the master. Doesn't say much, old Ramsey, but when he does, 'tis best to listen."

With a wink at the two rats, Duncan vanished down the hole. The bagpipes stopped abruptly.

The rat brothers sat close together for warmth. At home in San Francisco, it was early spring. But here it was still winter—cold and damp, with a few dirty snowdrifts in the shadows. Frederick knew they were much farther north than they'd ever been before—almost as far north as Alaska! It was a dizzying thought.

The loch shimmered under the starry sky. Frederick saw a sleek, sinuous shape rise—like the humped back of an enormous snake. It undulated across the surface in a serpentine series of loops and sank out of sight, leaving a V-shaped wake. An otter? Nessie? Frederick's ears perked. Beside him, Ishbu yawned and stretched.

"Think there'll be anything to eat, Freddy?" he said, leaning close. His whiskers tickled Frederick's ear.

Before Frederick could answer, Duncan's masked face peered up at them from the hole in the bank. He beckoned.

Should they follow? Frederick's nerves jangled. He thought of how angry the badgers had been at their first encounter. But he could face the most ferocious of badgers if they could help him find

Natasha and the professor.

Suddenly, an owl screamed. Ishbu yelped with fright and plunged into the pitch-black hole.

"Wait for me!" cried Frederick, leaping after him.

SEVEN BOLD BADGERS

THE TUNNEL WOUND DOWN INTO the earth. The rats followed Duncan until they entered a spacious den, much bigger than any room in his sett. Voices rumbled when the rats appeared. The six badgers sounded like a hundred. They stopped arguing and glared at the newcomers.

"Against oor better judgment, Dooncan has persuaded us t' listen to ye," said Angus. He jutted out his red-brown jaw. "So let's hear it."

"Sit doon, Angus," said Sandy calmly (Frederick recognized him from Duncan's description). "Let them talk."

Duncan quickly introduced the six badgers and motioned Frederick and Ishbu to a platform at one end of the hall. A red flag, with a design like the one in Duncan's sett, hung above them. Frederick felt every eye upon him. His knees knocked, and he took a steadying breath. He remembered Miss Dove's advice to her class—imagine your audience smiling at you—but picturing the sharp and shining teeth of seven grinning badgers did not reassure him.

Frederick cleared his throat and told his story. When he finished, there was silence for the space of three seconds, and then raised voices, pounding fists, stamping feet.

Don't they ever stop arguing? wondered Frederick. *How do they ever get anything done?*

"Brothers, a council o' war!" Duncan shouted. "These rats might succeed where we have failed."

"I'll not permit rats knowin' oor business," growled Angus. "'Tis for only the Brotherhood t' know."

"Aye!" cried Niall. "Badgers for badgers. And no ootsiders."

"Would ye then doom the professor, after all he's done for beasts? Doom him for the sake o' pride?" thundered Duncan.

"Pride!" shouted MacDuff. "Have ye no pride yerself? Oor clan needs no help!" He bared his teeth. "Not from puny rats. The guards will make mincemeat o' them! Why, I could break both their backs wi' a single snap!"

"That's why we must work together," said Duncan. "We provide the brawn, whilst they provide the"—he looked at the rats as if trying to figure out exactly what they might provide. Frederick straightened up and tried to look brave. Ishbu didn't bother.

"—the brains," finished Duncan, somewhat uncertainly. "You heard their story."

"Nae!" cried Niall. "We fight the low-bellied scum o' the Big Cheese oorselves!" He looked ready to attack immediately, and Ishbu cowered a bit behind Frederick.

"Duncan's plan has some merit, seein' as how the rats are wee creatures and can climb—," began Sandy in a reasonable tone, but he was shouted down by Angus and Niall.

"We need no help from vermin," scoffed Brock. "Look at them—they don't look big enough to whip an earthworm!"

"That's jist why they might succeed!" said Duncan. "And they can be taught to fight like badgers."

Niall bristled. "You'd have us give away oor fightin' secrets, too?"

"It's a badger-eat-badger world oot there." Duncan pointed at Frederick. "They've proved they're nae cowards. For the professor's sake, I say we give them whit help we can. Initiate them into the Ancient Brotherhood, train them in oor ways. Wi' a badger's heart and a badger's know-how, they may triumph where we failed."

There was more shouting at this.

"Well, Ramsey?" Duncan turned to the oldest badger, a fat, shaggy boar who had as yet said nothing. "Whit say you?"

The other badgers quieted, waiting for Ramsey's reply.

"Take a vote," Ramsey said.

"Aye! A vote, a vote!" The room rumbled with agreement.

"Vote aye to initiate these friends of Professor Ratinsky as honorary members of the Ancient Brotherhood of Badgers!" announced Duncan.

"And vote nae if ye think we should throw them int' the loch like the vermin they are and save the professor oorselves!" growled Angus.

As they talked, Frederick realized what a tightly knit group the Brotherhood was. They might disagree, but in the end they worked together.

"So be it," declared Duncan.

At once every badger became still and solemn, and Frederick had the sense that he was witnessing an oft-repeated ritual. Ramsey and MacDuff rambled down the center aisle to a chest at the rear of the hall. The badgers returned with a carved wooden box and set it on the platform near the rats. The box had a hole in the top.

One by one, each badger walked up to the platform and dropped something into the box. Frederick heard the clink of stone, like a pebble falling. Duncan leaned over and said in a low tone, "Black for nae, and white for aye."

When each badger, including Duncan, had voted, Ramsey and MacDuff opened the box and pulled out the stones. They sorted the pebbles into two piles, white and black. Frederick could see five white pebbles, two black. They were in!

Then his face fell. For what, exactly, did it mean to be initiated?

He and Ishbu would soon find out. . . .

THE INITIATION

THE CEREMONY BEGAN IMME-diately. Ishbu begged for a meal or even a snack. The two rats hadn't eaten since Duncan's tea. "Nothing?" asked Ishbu sadly.

Duncan glowered at them. "Ye must fast. 'Tis the custom. If ye want to be a badger, ye must learn to do as we do. Often in winter, when food is scarce, we do without."

Ishbu nodded, but his tummy grumbled.

The rats waited outside the meeting hall while the badgers prepared for the ceremony. Then Duncan came to get them. Brock stood guard at the hall entrance. Duncan gave the password: "Never give up."

"Never let go," Brock answered. Duncan blindfolded the rats, and Brock stood aside to let them pass.

Once inside the hall, Frederick heard the sound of paws drumming on the earthen floor. He smelled the musky scent of boars, and his fur bristled. It still went against his instincts to be so close to so many omnivores, but he thought of Natasha and steeled his courage.

The drumming grew louder. Frederick and Ishbu were given mugs of some strong, fizzy drink. It was like nothing Frederick had ever tasted. It made him woozy, and his head swam.

"Can I have some more, please?" asked Ishbu.

"Silence!" said one of the badgers. (Frederick thought it was Angus.) "The candidates do not speak." The badger growled and continued, "First, the presentation of the candidates. Then the tasks. Last, the oath of loyalty." He chuckled and added ominously, "*If* they pass."

Angus (after catching a whiff, Frederick was quite sure) led the blindfolded rats around the burrow. Every few paces Angus stopped, and something feathery and pungent hit them in the face. Frederick smelled a dusty, weedy scent. He thought it might be fronds of heather. After the first time, he knew what to expect and didn't flinch but squared his shoulders and met the blows head on. It felt like being slapped with a scratchy feather duster.

Three times they circled the room to the beat of drumming paws. They stopped in the center. Frederick could hear and smell the badgers grouped all around him.

"Noo the tasks," growled Angus. "And woes

betide any candidate who fails!"

Angus removed their blindfolds and led them outside, followed by the rest of the Brotherhood. They stood under the gnarled thorn tree, its branches twisted against the night sky like grasping fingers. The badgers weren't arguing now. They stared at the rats with steady, serious eyes.

"There are five tasks," said Duncan. "Five trials ye must pass t' join the Ancient Brotherhood of Badgers. It isna every badger who can do them. Only the bravest, strongest, wisest badgers can belong."

"First task," said Angus, "ye must excavate a burrow fifty paces long and as wide as a badger, for badgers are excellent diggers."

The two rats began, and after an hour, had excavated a burrow as long as fifty rat paces and as wide as two rats snuggled side by side. Frederick's paws were sore, and Ishbu had blisters. Neither of them had ever dug a burrow before.

Angus and Brock sniffed the burrow, crammed their big bodies inside as far as they could, and measured it with their paws. Angus grunted. "'Tis nae fit for a badger, but I guess 'twill do for rats."

The badgers circled around the rats until MacDuff stood in front of them. The starlight made the broad stripes on his face into a sinister mask. "Second task," he intoned, "ye must find and eat two hundred earthworms each, for badgers have enormous appetites." He smacked his lips. (In spite of his own enormous appetite, Ishbu looked a little green.)

Fortunately, the night was damp and still, or the two rats would never have found enough worms. Even so, it took hours. The crescent moon had risen well above the ruins when they presented the four hundred earthworms to MacDuff.

Eating them was another matter. Although both Frederick and Ishbu enjoyed the rubbery texture and chewy earthiness of an occasional worm, Frederick pointed out to the badgers that two hundred apiece would make even Ishbu too sick to finish the initiation. MacDuff consented to let them off with twelve apiece. He stored the rest under a pile of wet leaves. "For the feast later," he told them, "provided ye pass."

The badgers circled again, and this time Sandy stopped in front of the rats. "Third task," he said in his quiet voice, "ye must follow oor trail and mark it with yoor scent glands. 'Tis how the other clans recognize oor territory."

Following the badgers' trail to the meeting hall was a simple task for Frederick and Ishbu. Unlike the badgers, who marked their territory by rubbing their bottoms up against trees, the rats rubbed their sides and shoulders against the trunks as they passed. The brothers scurried from tree to tree along the badger trail. Sandy snuffled and nodded.

The badgers circled once more, and now Niall stood in front of the rats, showing his wickedly sharp teeth. "Four. Ye must bite me and hold on, for a badger is known for tenacity. 'Never give up, never let go' is oor motto."

Frederick gaped at the brawny badger. Bite him? Frederick and Ishbu had been bred for children to handle. Biting was against their code of honor.

"Pretend I'm yoor worst enemy!" urged Niall. "Sink yoor teeth inta me!"

Frederick visualized the Big Cheese and nipped.

Despite his sharp teeth and powerful jaw muscles (for his size), his bite couldn't compare to the bite of a badger.

"Coom now!" urged Niall, easily shaking Frederick loose. "Ye must do better than that! Badgers are known for their gruesome bite. Have ye nae heard the expression 'as bold as a badger'?"

"I thought it was 'as bald as a badger,'" said Ishbu.

"Nae indeed! Whit would be the meaning o' that?" asked Niall.

Ishbu looked pointedly at the boar's backside, where his fur had worn bare from battles and scratching against tree stumps, but he wisely withheld comment.

Try as they might, neither Frederick nor Ishbu could hold on to the huge badger. The heavy, thick coat covering Niall's neck and shoulders proved impenetrable, and the wily badger was too quick to let them near his vulnerable backside.

The rats lay on the ground, panting and sweaty. They had failed.

Frederick closed his eyes. *What will become of Natasha and Professor Ratinsky now?*

NEVER LET GO

NIALL GRINNED, AS IF HE KNEW what Frederick was thinking. His teeth glinted in the moonlight. Frederick rolled over, nudged Ishbu to his feet, and wracked his brain for a way to hold on to a badger four times his size. Finally, the barest inkling of an idea came to him. His ears trembled as he tried not to look at Niall's teeth. Would it work? There was nothing to do but try!

So while Niall laughed, Frederick sprang at the badger, leaping completely over his head and landing on his thick shoulders. "Get down here where I can see ye!" roared Niall. But Frederick burrowed his nose into the badger's fur and chomped him in the tender place behind his ear. Frederick hoped Ishbu would follow his lead and attack while they had the element of surprise on their side.

"Foul!" yelled Niall. "That's nae allowed!" He

threw himself on the ground to try to crush Frederick beneath his weight. Ishbu now realized what Frederick intended. He leaped on Niall and sank his teeth into the thin fur on Niall's exposed stomach.

Niall rolled across the clearing with Frederick clinging to his back and Ishbu clamped to his belly. Ishbu's whole body shook as Niall flung him from side to side. Frederick's jaws ached from the strain of hanging on. Niall rose to his feet, gasping.

When Frederick and Ishbu realized that the badger had stopped fighting, they released their hold and dropped to the ground. Frederick rubbed his jaw. He thought he'd loosened a tooth.

"They cheated," Niall growled. Some of the other badgers chirred their displeasure.

"Nae," said Ramsey calmly. "The wee beasties used whit talents they have. They used their wits. A badger attacked by a bigger creature would do the same." The other badgers slowly nodded, and Niall reluctantly joined in.

Brock now faced the rats. "Fifth task," he said.

Frederick breathed raggedly. He was exhausted and knew Ishbu was, too. He imagined the fifth task must be the worst trial of all—capturing a Scottish wildcat? Lassoing the Loch Ness monster? Parachuting from the top of the tower? How would they ever pass?

He was surprised when the white tips of Brock's ears turned pink. Brock coughed a bit to cover his embarrassment. "Ye must dance the Badger Fling," he said. "'Tis the custom," he added, somewhat defensively.

"The Badger Fling!" cried Ishbu. "Freddy, you know I can't dance!" Frederick hushed him, and they turned to watch Brock and the others.

The Badger Fling was danced on four paws and was as much a drumming song as a dance. The badgers pounded the beat as Frederick and Ishbu kept time with their tiny pink paws.

Frederick recognized the stirring words of Robert Burns as Ramsey sang in a voice rusty with age: "Tyrants fall in every foe! Liberty's in every blow! Let us do or die!"

They whirled and twirled, nodding and bowing to one another, prancing in time to Ramsey's singing and Duncan's tuneful humming. The pounding of their feet echoed through the woods. Frederick and Ishbu spun and stamped, tossing their tails under the golden moon. When the moon set behind the woods, the badgers led the tired rats in to the meeting hall.

"The oath," said Duncan.

The two rats stood and raised their right paws, repeating the oath after Ramsey, the master badger. "On our honor," they chanted, "we do solemnly swear to uphold the mission of the Ancient

Brotherhood of Badgers. To honor its laws. To obey the master badger. To keep the secrets of the Brotherhood. To serve, to protect, and to prevail."

The ceremony ended with the motto "Never give up, never let go" and the secret paw clasp.

"We have t' make some concessions here," Duncan commented as he showed the rats the paw clasp. "Yoor paws are nowhere near big enough to do it right."

The ceremony was finished! MacDuff fetched the rest of the earthworms. From some unseen storage room, Sandy brought out bottles of icy ginger beer, while Brock and Niall carried in platters of shortbread and oatcakes. The seven badgers and the two new honorary badgers feasted until dawn.

Now to find the professor. And Natasha.

THE MISSION

"Noo that ye're officially members o' the Brotherhood," said Duncan, "I can tell ye whit we know."

They were once again in Duncan's sett. The rest of the badgers had crawled off to sleep in their own setts.

"The Big Cheese has returned to Scotland," Duncan went on. "Time and again oor Brotherhood has tried to unearth his Scottish headquarters—and failed. We've tried to crack his codes—and failed. We've tried to identify his spies—and failed."

"What about Natasha?" Frederick interrupted.

Duncan held up a paw. "Finally, we've tried to infiltrate his organization and—"

"—failed," finished Ishbu.

"Whit makes ye think so, laddie?" Duncan winked gleefully.

"You have spies in the Bilgewater Brigade?" asked Ishbu, still munching a piece of shortbread from the feast.

"Aye," said Duncan. "I could nae tell ye this afore, but whilst Ishbu was in a coma, we received word from oor lodge up north. The Big Cheese holds two prisoners in the dungeon at Aberglen Castle, many miles from here. One is the professor." He paused to take a sip of tea. "And the other is his daughter."

"Natasha!" cried Frederick. For a moment his heart sang, knowing she was still alive. Then the full meaning of Duncan's news hit him. "Prisoners!" he repeated. He glared at Duncan. "You've known this, and you've left them there to rot?"

"Nae, laddie," said Duncan. "We made an attempt to release them. But the dungeon entrance is too small for big-boned beasts such as oorselves."

"Can't you dig them out?" asked Ishbu. He glanced at Duncan's big paws and said admiringly, "Badgers must be able to dig through anything."

Duncan beamed with pride. Then his face fell. "Dig we did, but the professor and the lassie are imprisoned in the oubliette."

"What's that?" asked Ishbu.

Frederick answered, remembering an old encyclopedia page that once lined their cage. "It's a kind of dungeon. The only entrance is a trapdoor in the ceiling. *Oubliette* means 'cast aside' or 'forgotten' in French." He gulped at the thought of Natasha in such a place—cold, damp, hungry—*forgotten*.

Duncan nodded. "In Scotland, 'tis also known as

a bottle dungeon, being the shape o' a bottle. This particular one is carved into the rock itself." He paused. "Even badgers cannot dig through solid rock and—mind ye—the dungeon is guarded."

"We can't give up!" cried Frederick.

"I dinnae say we're giving up!" Duncan shouted. He recovered and began speaking again, more quietly. "In medieval times, prisoners were dropped down from the guardroom in the tower. The opening beneath the trapdoor is covered with an iron grate. 'Tis too heavy for the strongest of badgers to move, and the spaces between the iron bars are too narrow for the leanest of badgers to fit through. The Brotherhood talked of enlisting a snake to slither through the grate, but some claimed snakes are not t' be trusted and 'twas voted down."

Ishbu shuddered at the mention of snakes.

"Next we considered a shrew, but 'tis well known ye can't rely on a shrew to pay attention to the task at hand." Duncan looked at them. "Ye see where I'm goin', do ye not?"

Ishbu nodded slowly. "A rat could slip through."

"And rats can climb!" exclaimed Frederick, leaping to his paws. "Badgers can't climb, but rats can!"

Frederick and Duncan grinned at each other—united in dreams of rescue, glory, adventure.

But Ishbu quivered from head to tail. "Freddy," he whispered, "I'm scared."

CROSSING THE HIGHLANDS

IT WAS NO SMALL MATTER FOR TWO rats and seven badgers to journey across the Scottish Highlands. They spent the rest of the day preparing for the trip. (Ishbu prepared by eating enough for four rats.)

"There's an abandoned sett on the east bank o' Loch Ness," Duncan told them as they gathered supplies. "It runs beneath the forest. 'Twas built by badgers centuries ago, but now 'tis used only in times of trouble. Once there, we can travel underground wi' no one the wiser."

But first, they had to cross the loch.

They left at nightfall. The sky glowed pale green behind the trees as the two rats and Duncan met the others at the thorn tree. Wood pigeons cooed in the deepening dusk. One by one, the badgers and the rats slipped into the chilly waters of Loch Ness. They swam in a line, one behind the other. A person standing on the bank might have mistaken the row of rounded backs for the looped humps of the famed monster.

The badgers swam with their noses up, paddling like dogs with their strong legs. With their shorter legs and smaller paws, Frederick and Ishbu had to work hard to keep up, especially Ishbu. His arms and legs thrashed aimlessly as he struggled to keep his head above the water. Once, he swallowed a big gulp and choked.

"Hang on to my tail," Frederick told him. "I'll keep you afloat." Ishbu let Frederick tow him.

When they reached the east bank, the animals climbed ashore, shook themselves from head to foot, and headed overland, the badgers snuffling the earth to find the hidden entrance to the ancient sett. In a short time they located it, although the entrance was overgrown with bracken. MacDuff held the ferns aside so the rats could enter.

When they were underground, they traveled for hours in near silence in the tunnels, stopping only to forage for food and water. Sometimes, their route was blocked by roots or landslides, and they had to dig their way through. Ishbu's toenails wore down to the nubs from digging, and Frederick wondered if they would ever arrive at the end.

At last, Duncan grunted and pointed his nose to an exit hole. Frederick could see a bit of moonlight and smell fresh air. The group scrambled up and out.

They emerged in a thick wood, filled with trees and plants that Frederick had read about but never seen: beech, aspen, rowan, wych elm, and holly. A herd of red deer scattered as the badgers waddled through. Patches of snow still clung to shady places beneath the bare trees.

A fox barked, and Frederick's fur rose. What were a couple of pet rats doing out in the Highland woods in the middle of the night?

"My heart's in the Highlands a-chasing the deer," he whispered, remembering the plane ride with Natasha—beautiful, clever Natasha—and he pulled himself together.

MacDuff had slung a coil of rope over his shoulder, borrowed from a nearby farm. "This way," he grunted. "We've marked the trail."

"Lead on, MacDuff," said Duncan.

The badgers and rats padded silently behind MacDuff through the moonlit wood.

After several miles they came to a stream. "Follow the burn," said Ramsey. "It leads to the castle."

"Follow the *what*?" said Ishbu.

"The stream," said Duncan. "Hush now, we're getting close."

They nosed downhill along the banks of the stream until they broke out of the wood.

Straight ahead loomed the massive bulk of the castle.

ABERGLEN CASTLE

UNLIKE URQUHART CASTLE, ABER-glen wasn't a ruin but an imposing stone castle still used as a home by the thane of Aberglen and his family.

The group gathered beneath the wall, hidden in the bare stalks of the flower garden.

"Be wary, lads," murmured Brock. "The family is away, but there are always humans aboot—gardeners, servants, gamekeepers, that sort."

A rosy streak in the eastern sky told them night was coming to an end. How long had they traveled? One night? Several? Frederick had lost all track of time in the underground caverns. The wood behind them filled with melodic birdsong. Dawn couldn't be far off.

A heated (but whispered) discussion raged among the elder badgers: Ramsey, Duncan, and MacDuff.

Should they attempt the rescue now—with daylight coming on—or wait for the cover of darkness?

"Now!" squeaked Frederick, ignoring the rules of order. "We've waited long enough. Suppose Natasha or her father is hurt? Suppose they haven't any food or water? I didn't come this far to wait any longer!"

"This wee beastie has a badger's courage," said MacDuff approvingly. "So be it. We'll draw off the guards and keep them in the castle's maze whilst Frederick rappels into the bottle dungeon to rescue the prisoners. We'll take the fat rat with us to act as lookout."

Ishbu bristled a bit at "fat rat." He might have gained a few ounces with all the shortbread he'd eaten, but he was sure he'd lost weight on their cross-country trek.

Duncan took charge. "Ramsey, ye're the heaviest. Anchor the rope in the guardroom. Brock, ye're the quickest. Draw the guards from the tower outside to the maze. The rest o' us will lie in wait in the hedges o' the maze and deal wi' the dogs there."

Ishbu's ears shot up. "Dogs? Real dogs? Or is that another Scottish expression?"

Angus's lips drew back and he snarled. "Real dogs, laddies! The kind that bite. The kind man has oft' used for the wicked sport o' badger-baiting. Rat terriers, to be exact."

"Snip and Snarl!" exclaimed Frederick.

Duncan raised his brows. "Friends o' yours?"

"We've met," said Frederick grimly.

The badgers split up, slipping away under the foliage with Ishbu scampering to keep up. Brock headed directly for the guardroom. Frederick and Ramsey went the back route, around the castle, to stay out of Brock's way.

In the pearly dawn light, Frederick saw a red sandstone tower surrounded by a stone wall. Frederick and Ramsey crawled beneath the iron portcullis and scrambled over the open drawbridge. Ramsey led him through a chink in the wall into the castle. They slunk up the steps toward the guardroom.

Frederick could hardly believe he was inside a castle like the ones in the tales he loved. *Robin Hood!* *King Arthur!* Of course, the castle didn't look the way it would have in the Middle Ages—no guards armed with crossbows, no knights in shining armor, no vats of boiling oil. . . .

Frederick paused to peek through an arrow slit to see the courtyard below and spotted a shiny-booted chauffeur washing a Rolls-Royce. He sighed in disappointment, then remembered he was about to rescue a damsel in distress. "Faster," he urged.

Ramsey waddled down the corridor, snuffling the ground as he went. A loud volley of barking came from the garden, followed by a high-pitched kecker.

"That's the signal," Ramsey said. "Brock's got the

dogs away. Quick, noo."

They entered the guardroom, and Frederick was surprised to find nothing in it but the wooden trapdoor. But of course, no humans used it anymore; it was there only to show visitors.

Ramsey and Frederick pulled on the iron ring of the trapdoor. At first, it wouldn't budge, but then, with a groan, the door opened.

"That's it," Ramsey said, pointing to the iron grate just below. "Let's git it done." He slung the coil of rope from his shoulder and knotted one end to the grate. The other end he looped around his ample girth, and he began to play out the rope down through the grate.

Frederick leaned over and caught the whiff of stale air. He gazed into the inky interior.

"Natasha!" he called hoarsely. "I've come to save you!" (In his excitement, he forgot to mention the professor or to include Ishbu and the others.)

There was no answer. *Perhaps they're asleep*, thought Frederick. He peered again into the gruesome, dank, and airless pit. . . .

THE BATTLE OF THE BADGERS

When badgers fight,
then everyone's a foe

—John Clare

"READY," GRUNTED RAMSEY. HE leaned back, bracing himself.

Frederick's ears twitched as he heard the barking dogs and squealing keckers of the badgers.

"Hurry, laddie," warned Ramsey. "The badgers can nae hold the dogs off for long."

Frederick squeezed between the iron bars of the grate. He grasped the rope. The coarse fibers bit into his paws. He wrapped his hind feet and tail around the rope and slid into darkness.

Finally, his feet touched the floor. He looked up, and twenty feet above him—as high as a skyscraper to a rat—he saw the squares of light in the grate and Ramsey's striped face peering down at him.

"Natasha? Professor?" Frederick called. Still no answer.

The dungeon was empty.

Meanwhile Ishbu had followed the badgers to the maze. The plan was simple: lure the dogs into the maze and keep them away from the guardroom as long as possible.

"Aye," Angus said. "Keep 'em or kill 'em, whitever." He spat. "If ye ask me, killing's best."

The castle maze was a series of tall hedges growing close together, full of twists and turns and dead ends. Ishbu scrambled into the branches of an old beech tree, high enough to have a good view inside the maze but low enough to scamper down quickly. From there he could act as a lookout and warn the others when Brock brought the dogs.

He didn't have long to wait. Brock charged down the path from the castle, keckering loudly. Ishbu was astounded a badger could run so fast. Right behind him bounded the two rat terriers, snapping and barking.

"Here they come!" squealed Ishbu.

Brock led the dogs inside the outer circle of the maze and then slipped into the thicket of hedge to rest. Niall burst from his hiding place to tease the dogs, leading them farther inside.

From his perch in the tree, Ishbu watched the whole thing unfold. On their journey, the badgers had worked out a strategy. One at a time, the badgers engaged the dogs, taking turns leading them farther into the center of the maze. As each badger passed the hiding place of the next, he slipped off for a rest, then hid farther inside while a fresh badger took his place.

The dogs were never certain if they were following one badger or a thousand. If Frederick had been watching, he would have recognized it as a strategy worthy of the great Scottish hero William "Braveheart" Wallace himself! But Ishbu knew only that their plan was working.

Or so it seemed for a while. But all too soon, the dogs wised up. When it was Sandy's turn, instead of chasing him, the dogs backed off and stood a short distance away, refusing to be drawn any farther into the maze. Snip growled. Snarl narrowed his eyes.

"Whit ye waitin' for?" taunted Sandy, trying to get the terriers to follow. "Lily-livered louts!" The badger lowered his head between his front paws.

Suddenly, Snarl charged while Snip circled behind. Sandy whirled and swept his head up, knocking Snip to the side. Snarl went right for Sandy's ears, ripping and tearing one. Blood dripped down Sandy's tawny coat. Snip recovered and attacked from the rear.

Sandy howled in pain. The other badgers gave up their plan and rushed out of hiding to Sandy's aid.

The badgers attacked, but now the dogs changed tactics. The dogs stood their ground, circling the badgers, darting at them, nipping and barking. The dogs seemed to be everywhere at once. The badgers stood back to back, trying not to leave any side exposed.

Ishbu realized the dogs were deliberately herding the badgers out from the center of the maze, back into the open, back toward the castle!

And he could tell the badgers were tiring. They weren't built for sustained combat, and the long cross-country trek had taken its toll. Duncan's breath rasped. Snarl bit him in the leg, and he went down. All at once, both dogs charged MacDuff, and he screamed. Snip got him by the throat and shook him. MacDuff fell heavily to the ground.

Niall clamped his teeth onto Snarl's lower jaw. Snip leaped onto his back and bit him above the eye. Niall let go, and instantly both dogs attacked.

Angus and Brock ran to Niall's aid, but the dogs released Niall and jumped on Angus. Angus rolled over and over, trying to shake them loose. Finally, he grunted and stopped moving.

The badgers were falling. Ishbu didn't know what to do. Run and get Frederick and Ramsey? Stay put and try to help? He trotted back and forth along the beech limb, squeaking in frustration.

The battle raged directly beneath Ishbu's perch. Only Brock and Niall, the youngest badgers, were still on their feet. Snip grabbed Brock's leg. Ishbu heard the crunch of teeth against bone.

With a howl of rage, Brock slashed Snip across his ribs, leaving five bloody stripes. Yelping, Snip ran off, pursued by Sandy, who had recovered enough to give chase.

Snarl had Niall down on his back now. Niall screamed as Snarl went for his belly, the most vulnerable part of a badger. Ishbu couldn't wait any longer. Even though Frederick was the brave one, the adventurer, the hero, Ishbu found a courage he didn't know he had. He dove from the tree branch and landed with all four paws on Snarl's spine. He fastened his tiny, sharp incisors on Snarl's ear and chomped. Snarl howled and released his hold on Niall. The dog whipped from side to side, trying to shake the rat loose.

"Hang on, laddie! Hang on!" Ishbu heard one of the badgers cry. "Dinnae let go; we've almost got him!"

Ishbu closed his eyes and fastened his teeth tighter while the terrier bucked and rolled. Ishbu's teeth rattled, and his ears shook.

"Hold fast! A badger never lets go!" cried Niall as he sprang to his feet. Niall swiped the terrier's hind legs with his claws. Snarl fell to the ground. Duncan, still bleeding from his wounded leg, quickly sat on Snarl to prevent his escape. Ishbu released his hold, spit out a tooth, and crawled free, rubbing his jaw. It was completely numb.

"Ishbu!" Brock cried, limping over. He pounded Ishbu on the back so hard, the rat stumbled. "Ye did good, laddie! Lookit—we've captured one o' the enemy! Ye're a hero!"

Ishbu beamed. But then he noticed the winded, wounded badgers lying limp around him. The battle was over. But who had really won?

IN THE RAT HOLE

"If they're nae there, coom up," Ramsey called down into the bottle dungeon. "I think I hear someone."

"Just a minute," said Frederick. "I want to look around. Maybe they left a clue."

The floor was damp from centuries of water seeping in through the stone. The only light fell in thin shafts that barely penetrated the gloom, but Frederick used his nose. He followed the scent to a moldy, half-gnawed piece of Swiss cheese that lay near the wall. Someone had been here! And not long ago!

He called to Ramsey to tell him what he'd found, only to hear a muffled yelp from overhead. Frederick looked up and saw a whiskered face peering down at him. Not Ramsey's. A white face with black spots. Cruel eyes. Pointed teeth.

"Good-bye, sucker!" called Snip.

The trapdoor slammed shut.

∞

In the shelter of the maze, Ishbu and the badgers regrouped. The sun was now fully up, bringing all the dangers that came with daylight. They had to go underground, but as yet, no one had the strength.

Sandy waddled back into the maze, licking his wounds. "The other beast got away," he reported. Sandy's fur was clotted with blood. Altogether, the badgers looked the worse for wear. But they hadn't given up.

Duncan, still sitting on Snarl, grabbed him by the collar and growled, "Tell us whit ye know o' the Big Cheese's plans an' we'll go easy on ye."

Snarl thrust out his jaw defiantly and laughed in Duncan's face. "You won't get anything outta me," he said. He struggled but couldn't free himself. The badger outweighed him. "You chumps are too late!" Snarl bragged. "The Big Cheese has flown the coop. He's won, in spite of you and that pesky rat!" He glared at Ishbu. The tips of Ishbu's ears grew warm, and he grinned modestly—really, he'd hardly done anything.

Snarl hesitated for a moment. "We thought both you rats were dead. You shoulda drowned. . . ." He shook his head. "It don't matter. The Boss stole the pearls and split."

"Pearls?" said Niall, looming over the terrier. One

eye was swollen shut, but the badger still looked dangerous. "Ye would nae be talking aboot Scotland's famous freshwater mussel pearls, would ye?" His voice was low, but Ishbu heard the threat behind it.

"That's illegal!" cried Duncan. "Those mussels are endangered!"

"Who cares?" replied Snarl, struggling again. "The Big Cheese don't give a rip for human laws. Why should he? What have humans ever done for us animals?" Duncan gripped the dog's collar more firmly. Snarl stopped thrashing and lay still. "Search all ya want. He's gone. The professor and the girl, too."

"Back to San Francisco?" guessed Ishbu. "Chinatown?"

Snarl laughed triumphantly. "He's got a new headquarters now. Too high for the likes of you. Flies with the cuckoos, he does. Nests with the eagles, climbs with the mountain goats. You'll never find him. Or his factory, either."

With that, Snarl gave a sudden twist and slipped out of his collar. Before Duncan could react, the dog had wriggled from underneath him and dashed under the hedge. The badgers heard him barking mockingly in the distance.

Brock charged after the terrier but came back a few minutes later. "The scoundrel got away."

Ishbu picked up Snarl's abandoned collar and

examined it, the way he knew Frederick would have if he'd been there. The collar was red leather. On the inside Ishbu saw some writing and, even though he couldn't read it, he recognized the letters.

He'd seen them before.

OB-LA-DI, OB-LA-DA, OUBLIETTE

WITH THE TRAPDOOR SHUT, NO AIR or light came into the pit. Worse yet, there was no hope.

But Frederick still had his instincts. His ancestors were used to confined alleys and the airless holds of ships, cellars and basements, sewers and tunnels. Frederick used his nose, his ears, and his whiskers—as sensitive as a moth's feelers—to guide him.

The first thing he did was to locate the rope still hanging from the grate above, the grate that was now sealed tight by the closed trapdoor. He scrambled up and shoved against the trapdoor with all his might. But a rat's might is no match for a heavy wooden door bound in iron, and it refused to budge. Dejected, Frederick slid back down the rope.

He crept around the perimeter of the narrow, circular pit, sniffing and rubbing his paws across the walls, feeling for a crack that might indicate a passage to the outside. He wasn't optimistic. But it was better than sitting hopelessly, preparing to die.

He tripped over something. Wondering what it could be, Frederick spread his forepaws across the clammy stone floor, searching . . . searching . . . and found a long, slender piece of metal, pointed at one end. He knew that shape! He stroked the metal surface and brought it to his nose. Perhaps only a nose as keen as Frederick's could have detected the faint fragrance of cinnamon still clinging to the metal. Natasha's nail file!

She must have dropped it.

A steel file could scratch sandstone, he thought. Perhaps Natasha had used her nail file to leave a message on the dungeon wall. Breathlessly, Frederick searched the walls again with eager paws, tracing cracks and chips. A few carvings met his delicate paw tips. A date—1509— gave him pause. Centuries ago, some poor soul had probably met a gruesome fate in this horrible place.

A bit lower, his paws found other scratchings, so worn they were barely legible. He painstakingly made out the letters as he read aloud. "Abandon hope, ye who enter here." Frederick wondered what had become of the prisoner who scratched *that* message.

'Round and 'round he went, his paws searching

the walls in the darkness. Most of the scratchings felt too old and worn—or too meaningless—to be a message from Natasha.

After a long search, Frederick found a row of letters that felt more recent: "Z," he spelled aloud, "E, R, M, A." And was that last letter an *H* or two *Ts*? "T, T," he decided. "Zermatt." Did it ring a faint bell? Perhaps it was someone's name. Or maybe he was merely dizzy from lack of food and water.

He found more scrapings. Was that a capital *N-A-T*? Would Natasha have scratched her name into the rock? Was she hoping that Frederick would somehow survive and find her?

Or did she believe herself beyond help and was simply passing the time as other prisoners had done, by scratching her name into the rock. He stroked the stone anxiously, but there was no more writing. Instead, something thick and still somewhat sticky covered the rest of the carving. He pressed his nose to it and inhaled . . . *blood*?

CLUELESS

"'Tis time to cut oor losses," MacDuff said. "Bind up the wounded. Head for the abandoned sett." The rest of the badgers shuffled painfully to their feet. "The others will meet us there."

Ishbu shook his head. "Not me. I'm going to find Frederick and Ramsey."

"I'll coom wi' ye, laddie," said Duncan. "Snip and Snarl may yet be on the prowl, and ye may need my protection." He bared his teeth and, despite his limp, he looked fierce.

Together they scrambled through the hedge, Duncan moving as fast as possible on his wounded leg. They edged closer to the castle walls, keeping watch. They ran into no more trouble, however, and soon reached the guardroom in the tower.

A furry mound lay on the floor. "Ramsey!" cried

Duncan, hurrying to him. Ishbu was relieved to hear the fallen badger moan. "Whit happened?" asked Duncan.

Ramsey rubbed his head and winced. "I've a knot as big as a goose egg. I dinnae see whit hit me."

The two badgers pulled the trapdoor open. Ishbu climbed on top of the grate. "Freddy!" he called. "Freddy?" He peered into the gloom.

Frederick climbed up the rope like a pirate with something as sharp and shiny as a dagger between his teeth.

"Are you okay? What happened?" asked Ishbu.

"Later," said Frederick. "It's too dangerous here."

"The laddie's right," said Duncan. "Let's meet the others at the old sett and have oor parley there."

They made their way back in record time. All the other badgers were moving about, having dug up a great pile of earthworms and found water somewhere and roots and berries. The hungry animals tucked in as though it were a victory feast and not a defeat.

But defeat it was.

Once they'd sated their hunger, the group compared notes.

"We learned something, did we nae?" said Angus, licking his sore paws.

"We did?" asked Ishbu.

"Whit was it the doggie said?" responded Brock.

"Something aboot eagles?"

"Like a riddle," said Sandy. "I dinnae catch it all."

"He bragged that the Big Cheese has gone somewhere 'too high' for us," said Duncan slowly. "Flies with the cuckoos. Nests with the eagles. Climbs with the mountain goats."

"Aye, so he did. But whit does it mean?" said Niall, slurping down the last earthworm.

"Mountain goats," mused Frederick. "Eagles. Cuckoos." He scratched his ears with his paw. "Well, eagles are found in the mountains, too. And there are cuckoos in Germany and Austria." He sighed. "I'm afraid that doesn't help much. Did he give anything else away?"

"Something aboot a new headquarters and a factory," piped up MacDuff. His voice was hoarse from the wound on his throat.

"Maybe he has a factory in the mountains? The Pyrenees, the Alps?" wondered Frederick. "But why would the Big Cheese need a factory?" He stroked Natasha's nail file while he talked.

Ishbu sat on the edge of the circle, munching roots and lending only half an ear to the discussion. He still basked in the glow of the badgers telling how he—brave Ishbu!—had ambushed Snarl and bit him just like a badger. If it hadn't been for him . . .

Ishbu jumped up. "I forgot about this!" He dragged forth the red leather collar that Snarl had left behind. "Look, Freddy! Look on the inside! That pet food company from the ad in the paper!"

Frederick examined the collar carefully and saw the stamped letters: TTPFCo. "Ishbu, you're right! Tasty Tails Pet Food Company! But how did you read it?"

"It's the same as on their label," Ishbu said. "The red and yellow one."

Frederick tried to visualize the pet food label from the ad in their cage, but he hadn't paid as much attention to it as Ishbu had. "Weren't there some other words, too?" he asked, furrowing his brow. "I remember 'Made in Switzerland.' But I don't see how that helps." He shrugged. "Maybe the company gives these collars away with their dog food."

"The pet food must be made in a factory," suggested Ishbu.

Frederick grabbed his brother. "Of course! Ishbu, you've done it! The Big Cheese has gone to a pet food factory in Switzerland!"

Ishbu grinned.

"Ye'll have to explain that one to us," said Sandy, shaking his head. "I dinnae follow."

"One," Frederick said, ticking off on his nails. "Snarl hinted the Big Cheese has a new headquarters —and a factory—someplace where there are eagles, cuckoos, and mountain goats. That could mean the Alps. Switzerland is in the Alps."

He spun on his heel and began to pace. "Two. I

found Natasha's nail file in the oubliette." He struggled to keep his emotions under control as he thought of the bloodstains. "Natasha scratched the word *Zermatt* on the dungeon wall. I didn't figure it out at first, but Zermatt is in Switzerland."

He turned to his brother. "Remember Miss Dove's geography lessons? The world map? The Matterhorn—the most famous mountain in the Swiss Alps—is located in Zermatt."

Ishbu blinked, recalling instead an empty box that Miss Dove had once put in their cage for a bed. It smelled of chocolates and (before he'd chewed it to bits), there had been a photo of a big, white mountain on the front.

"That could be what Natasha was trying to say," Frederick went on. "That the Bilgewater Brigade is taking them to Zermatt. To the new European headquarters of the Big Cheese and"—he paused dramatically—"the factory of the Tasty Tails Pet Food Company!"

The badgers looked puzzled, and Angus stamped his paw impatiently. "But why would the Big Cheese want a pet food company?"

"There's more," said Frederick, pivoting to pace in the other direction. "Ishbu told me about a newspaper article reporting weird pet behavior." He looked at Ishbu. "Wasn't it possibly connected to their food?"

Ishbu nodded.

Frederick continued. "Natasha's father was working on a formula. Something to do with cats and dogs. Pets. Weird behavior. Pet food made in Switzerland. The Big Cheese in the mountains, a factory of some kind . . . These things *must* add up somehow." It was a slim thread to hang a whole theory on, but it was all he had. He squared his shoulders. "We have to go to Zermatt and find the Tasty Tails Pet Food factory."

Suddenly Frederick's excitement ebbed. He sat down, his head in his paws. "Switzerland," Frederick moaned. "Hundreds of miles away! Ishbu, we aren't even in the right country. How are we ever going to get to Switzerland?"

HERRING BOAT TO NORWAY

TWENTY-FOUR HOURS LATER, THE RATS gripped the railing of a fishing trawler with all eight paws and both tails and watched the coastline of Scotland recede into the mist.

The speed at which events had progressed took Frederick's breath away. He thought back to yesterday, when they'd rendezvoused in the sett outside Aberglen Castle, and he had despaired.

But the badgers had offered a solution.

"The Brotherhood can help," said Duncan.

Frederick had raised his head hopefully. "How?"

"As I told ye, oor lodges extend across Europe. A word from me and ye'll have all the help ye need. Dinnae forget—ye're honorary members o' the Ancient Brotherhood of Badgers now."

"Will you come, too?" asked Ishbu. He'd grown fond of the badgers over the past few days.

"Nae, laddies. Oor work is here. Each lodge

protects its own territory. But ye'll be in good paws." Duncan paused a little self-consciously, then added, "Also, 'tis a well-known fact that Scottish badgers get horribly seasick."

"I know the feeling." Ishbu sighed.

"Use the signs to identify friends," said Duncan, reminding them of the A.B.O.B. secret passwords and paw clasp.

It had been hard to say good-bye, but they did, creeping on board the fishing trawler in the wee hours of the morning.

"Good luck to ye," said Angus. One by one, each badger saluted the rats and then melted into the fog.

Duncan had been the last to say good-bye. "Godspeed, laddies," he said. Frederick had been touched to see tears in the old boar's eyes (or maybe it was just the mist).

Now the trawler headed across the North Sea. The waves became rougher. Frederick stared out, watching orca whales glide and dolphins leap in the cold, black waters.

An icy wind whistled by the two rats. They headed belowdecks and curled up in the hold. It smelled strongly of herring. Ishbu, of course, was seasick.

Frederick stayed awake all night, listening to the slap of waves against the hull and the steady thrum of the engine. But nothing unusual happened, and when the boat docked at Stavanger, Norway, the two rats (one greenishly pale) scrambled across the ropes to land.

Lars, the master badger of Norway, met them on the dock. He put them up in his cozy sett and fed them lutefisk, a kind of pickled cod. Over the meal, Lars told them proudly how Norway rats —intrepid sailors like the Vikings—had colonized the entire world.

The next night, Lars helped them stow away on the ferry to Denmark. Ishbu huddled in the hold, sick and miserable again. This time, Frederick stayed on deck, clinging to the railing and watching the sky. The previous night's storm had blown over, and the lights of the aurora borealis were like a shimmering curtain in the black sky. In the face of everything —the danger, the discomfort, his terrible worry over Natasha—Frederick was having the adventure of a lifetime.

The master badger of Denmark met them at the ferry dock in a sheltered area. To their surprise, it wasn't a boar but a sow named Dagmar. She took them to her sett and fed them pickled herring and *rugbrød*, a rye bread.

Dagmar woke them early the next morning. "I've made all the arrangements," she said. "You're to hide between the crates in the rear of a delivery van. It travels from farm to farm. Hop off at the fifth farm after crossing the border into Germany. Take shelter beneath the old barn. The master badger of Germany will meet you there.

"Be wary of foxes and ferrets," she added. "This is farm country. Plenty of predators." Ishbu's eyes widened. Dagmar gave him a hearty slap on the back and smiled. "Don't trust anyone, and you'll be all right."

They followed Dagmar's directions and found the van parked in front of a bakery in the village near her sett. Fragrant smells wafted out to the street. Ishbu closed his eyes and inhaled blissfully. Frederick had to nip his paw to remind him of their mission.

They sneaked into the van. Ishbu hunkered down between the cardboard boxes as instructed, but Frederick found that by standing on a stack of crates and craning his neck, he could see out the rear window. From the angle of the sun, he could tell they were heading south.

Denmark was a pretty country of flat fields and tidy farms. Frederick knew they must be on the cusp of spring here (though he'd lost count of the days since they'd left the classroom), but the weather showed no signs of it yet. The fields lay damp and brown beneath gray skies. In a few hours, they crossed the border into Germany.

They jumped out of the van at the fifth farm. The old barn Dagmar told them about was straight ahead, a big half-timbered structure with a thatched roof. It was built on a stone foundation, and Frederick spied plenty of rat-size holes between the stones. Not wanting to be seen, the two rats took off at a run, rounded the corner of the barn . . . and came face-to-face with an enormous black cat.

FRIENDS AND FOES

 FREDERICK FROZE. ISHBU, NOT realizing Frederick had stopped, slid into him, nearly knocking him over. Ishbu went completely still, with only the tips of his whiskers quivering.

The cat stared at them, her green eyes unblinking and her ears cocked and alert.

Frederick's eyes darted to the barn. Could they make it to safety before the cat pounced?

Then he realized something very odd. Even though the cat stared right at them, crouched and tense as if to strike, she didn't appear to really see them.

It was almost as if the cat were hypnotized. Frederick tested his theory. He wriggled his ears. No response. He wiggled his nose. The cat didn't blink.

"Come on, Ishbu," he whispered to his brother,

who was cowering behind him, "let's—MOVE!" On the word *move*, the two rats sprinted for the barn and wedged themselves between the stones of the foundation. Once inside, Frederick put his eye to a crack and looked out. The cat remained fixed in position, still staring. She hadn't even turned to watch them run.

"Is it a real cat?" asked Ishbu when he'd caught his breath. "Or a statue or something?"

Frederick nibbled his toenails to calm himself. "It's real, all right. Can't you smell it?"

Ishbu wrinkled his nose. There was no mistaking that cat stink.

A slight cough came from behind them. Frederick scanned the shadows. Two badgers waited in the crawlspace. Frederick eyed them suspiciously. *Two badgers?* Dagmar hadn't mentioned that. "This may be a trap," he murmured to Ishbu. "Get ready to run again."

His fur bristled as he gave the password: "Never give up."

"Never let go" came the answer.

Frederick sighed with relief. Ishbu darted up and sniffed them and offered the secret paw clasp. Frederick clicked his teeth politely.

The German badgers were named Leopold and Wilhelm. They were brothers also. They took the rats through a tunnel that led from the barn to their sett.

"We have news for you," said Leopold, the master, offering them a plate of bockwurst sausage and black bread.

"News?" Ishbu struggled to keep his eyes open even as he munched. (He really was trying his best, but he was a homebody from the tip of his nose to the end of his tail. Adventures simply wore him out.)

"*Ja*," said Wilhelm, "we have heard reports of criminal activity. In Berlin, Paris, and Zurich. Burglaries, jewel thefts, smuggling. Fouled cargo. Contaminated food stores. And at the scene of the crime, always the paw prints of dogs. His trademark, we are thinking."

"The Big Cheese," said Frederick.

"Always one step ahead of us." Leopold scratched his chin.

After this disturbing news, the rats barely slept a wink.

The next evening, with the badgers' help, they boarded a barge that would take them up the Rhine River through Germany and into France.

From his knowledge of geography, Frederick guessed that their route was indirect at best and downright rambling at worst, but he kept his mouth shut. No one likes a complainer, and at least they were protected from foxes, weasels, ferrets, and—worst of all—rat terriers. He and Ishbu had a lot to be thankful for.

The vessel was a commercial barge, not a luxury boat, and several scruffy river rats were already aboard, gnawing on the wooden crates in the stern. Frederick gave them a wide berth. They looked tough.

Could they be members of the Bilgewater Brigade?

RHINE RIVER CRUISE

THEY SAILED AT DAWN. FREDERICK sat with his tail curled around his paws to keep them warm. The barge chugged up the river, passing steep, forested hills crowned with storybook castles and medieval fortresses, and rolling hills planted with vineyards, the vines still brown and bare. Frederick imagined the vines in summer— thick and green, dripping with luscious purple grapes. He smacked his lips. The steady thrum of the engine was hypnotic. The barge sailed smoothly. Even Ishbu couldn't get sick on this boat!

The barge passed romantic villages with cobblestone streets and modern cities with smoke-belching factories. They passed churches with tall, thin steeples or round onion domes and clock towers that chimed the hours.

The sun shone weakly through hazy clouds,

giving little warmth. Many boats were out on the river now. All sizes of craft—from enormous barges much bigger than theirs to sporty motorboats —zipped up and down. In the late afternoon, a cutting wind blew from the mountains, bringing the scent of snow and the sting of sleet. The river turned gray, and whitecaps sprang up. The pleasure boats turned for shore and safe harbors. Frederick shivered. It felt as if spring would never come.

They left the main river and nosed up a narrow channel, where bare branches trailed in the water. Frederick thought they might be in France now. The wind nipped his nose. He joined Ishbu in the shelter between the crates. His brother had made a nest of bits of fur, paper, and fluff. The wild rats were there, too, playing some game with pieces of straw.

"Olaf, Hans, Pierre," Ishbu introduced them. "Meet my brother, Freddy."

Trust Ishbu to make friends with anyone! The rats clicked their teeth in greeting.

"Not from around here, are you?" said one of the river rats. Frederick shook his head. The others spoke with strong accents that were hard to understand.

The wild rats left the barge at the next port. Frederick was sorry he'd misjudged them. It wasn't much fun to be suspicious of everyone.

Frederick and Ishbu disembarked in a village in France, where the German badgers had given them instructions to meet the French master, a chic young sow named Madeleine, on the bank.

Madeleine led the way to a snug pied-à-terre (as she called her burrow) concealed in the roots of an oak tree. They dined (by candlelight, no less) on truffles, ratatouille, endive, and chocolate mousse.

"Ratatouille for the rats!" joked Ishbu.

"I must warn you," Madeleine told them as they lingered over café au lait, "zee cats and dogs around here are acting very strange. Zat I have seen with my own eyes."

"How can you tell if a cat's acting weird?" asked Ishbu. "That's just the way they are."

"*Oui,*" said Madeleine, breaking off a piece of baguette and nibbling it delicately. "But zees pets don't come when called. Zee cats, of course, never did. But zee dogs are driving zere human masters crazy. Working dogs—rescue dogs, Seeing Eye dogs, fire dogs, sheep dogs, hounds. Even hunting dogs. Zee cats and dogs all stare into space, ears cocked, listening."

Madeleine crossed her eyes and stared at the ceiling—mouth open, head tilted, her expression vacant. Ishbu giggled. Then her face returned to normal, and she shrugged. "To what do zey listen?"

"Hey, we saw that in Germany," said Ishbu. "Remember the black farm cat, Freddy?"

"This must be part of the Big Cheese's plan," said

Frederick. "He's doing something to the cats and dogs. I'll bet it involves the professor's work. But what is it? And why? And where does Natasha fit in?" Saying her name made his heart ache. *Where is she? Is she even still alive?*

"Tomorrow, you will meet Fritz, ze Swiss master," said Madeleine.

"Good," said Frederick. "We're counting on him to help us find the factory. I just hope that I'm right and Natasha and her father are there. That's all that matters."

TRACKS IN THE SNOW

AFTER DINNER, MADELEINE LED THE rat brothers up a trail into the mountains. They were so far above the river that the barges below looked like toy boats. The air was chilly. Patches of snow lay on the ground. High above them, snow-capped mountains turned as pink as strawberry ice cream in the reflected light of the setting sun. "Alpenglow," Madeleine told them.

Before leaving, Madeline kissed each rat good-bye on both cheeks in the French fashion. "*Bonne journée,*" she said, wishing them a good trip.

Frederick and Ishbu spent the night in an empty sett in a cow pasture. They fell asleep to the tinkling sound of bells and the quiet munching of cows.

In the morning, they boarded a yellow Swiss postal bus, scrambling up the steps and darting past the driver before the passengers entered. They hid under the backseat. Madeleine had told them the bus would take them through the Swiss Alps as it delivered the mail.

The bus climbed along narrow roads that switched back and forth across the mountains. Poor Ishbu was bus sick. (It's especially hard to be a brave adventurer when you have motion sickness!) The bus traveled through tunnels and over bridges to villages and hamlets, stopping to load and unload packages, and to pick up and drop off passengers.

The snow deepened as they climbed the mountains. The branches of the fir trees were frosted with white—like glitter on a Christmas card. The sky burned blue.

The road narrowed to one track. The driver blew his horn before rounding corners to warn other vehicles of his approach. Frederick, feeling daring, hopped to the top of the empty backseat and gazed out the window. A cliff towered over the road on the right, the jagged snow-covered rocks hanging above them. The road shelved off steeply on the left, down to a thin, silver ribbon of river far below. Frederick wondered how often a rockslide or avalanche closed the road. His whiskers twitched nervously.

They disembarked in a valley. A cluster of brown chalets surrounded a church with a tall steeple. Everything was covered with snow.

Frederick recalled Madeleine's directions: up the

cow path to the granary, under the birch tree by the northeast corner. That's where they would find Fritz. They followed the cow tracks, taking care no humans noticed their passage.

It was a challenge to walk through the snowdrifts. The two rats jumped from one hoofprint to the next, trying to keep their bellies dry. When they realized they were light enough not to sink, they crept across the crust of snow, leaving faint paw prints. Their paws got chilled, and Ishbu stopped to nibble the ice balls that had formed between his toes.

The day, which had started out sunny, had clouded over. It began to snow—soft, minute flakes that tickled the rats' whiskers like butterflies.

The rats had never seen falling snow before, only pictures in Miss Dove's room. "It's much colder than it looks, isn't it?" Frederick said, his breath puffing out in a misty cloud.

Ishbu stuck out his pink tongue to taste the snowflakes. "Not much flavor, though," he noted.

They pushed on, following the trail through a belt of trees and into the high open country above the village. Frederick imagined the meadow in summer, covered with wildflowers as thick and colorful as a tapestry. So different from this forbidding expanse of white!

They found the granary easily enough, a wooden hut standing on top of stacked stone disks like a house on stilts. "That must be to keep the field mice from the grain," murmured Frederick.

"And the rats." Ishbu sighed. He was hungry again.

From a distance, the snow appeared velvety smooth, but on closer inspection, Frederick saw that there were tracks all around—bird tracks, badger tracks, and something else . . . dog prints! The tracks circled the granary. Frederick stared at them, and the fur rose along his neck. He followed the paw prints around the corner while Ishbu hung behind, snuffling something in the snow.

"Freddy, come quick!" Ishbu called.

Frederick raced over and saw Ishbu nudging a fur coat lying in the snow. Frederick sniffed. It wasn't a coat. It was the body of a badger, cold and stiff.

Punctured with the teeth marks of a rat terrier!

Part Three:
THE MOUNTAIN

Avenge, O Lord, thy slaughter'd saints, whose bones
Lie scatter'd on the Alpine mountains cold . . .
—John Milton

The best laid schemes o' mice an' men . . .
—Robert Burns

EDGAR

FREDERICK AND ISHBU DUG A grave fifty paces long and as wide as a badger. They respectfully buried the body of Fritz, the Swiss master, and covered it with snow. Then they bowed their heads for a moment of silence. When they finished, the rats took shelter beneath the granary. It was snowing hard now, thick clumps of loose, wet flakes falling from a steel-gray sky.

The chilled rats found a crevice in the stone disks and crawled in. Outside, the wind howled and blowing snow blocked their view.

They nestled together for warmth. They were heartsick that the Swiss badger had been killed. "As a member of the A.B.O.B., he knew the danger," said Frederick sadly as Ishbu dried his eyes with his tail. "He knew the risks. He died a hero."

Frederick stared outside at the swirling snow. He

had never felt so helpless in his life. They had no directions, no map, and no network of friendly badgers helping them on their way.

Even worse, somewhere out there roamed the minions of the Big Cheese. Frederick cringed at the thought of rat terriers, weasels, stoats, wharf rats, ferrets, and others—all intent on killing them. And then what would become of the professor and Natasha?

"We've got to get to Zermatt," said Frederick. "But how?"

"Zermatt?" croaked a voice overhead.

Frederick squinted up. A black feathered shape perched in the beams beneath the granary. *A raven.* The bird flew down and hopped over to the rats.

"My name is Edgar," he rasped.

"Like Edgar Allan Poe?" asked Frederick, remembering the spooky poems and stories Miss Dove had read.

"Not at all," said the raven huffily. "I can't tell you how often I hear that. Someone's always quoting 'nevermore' at me. Ravens foretelling death! Ha! I wish that fellow had written about vultures instead! Now *that* would have made sense!"

Frederick hurried to steer the raven back on topic. Maybe he had information that would help them. After all, birds flew long distances and knew the terrain well. "Do you know how to get to Zermatt?" Frederick asked.

"Why go to Zermatt?" asked Edgar. "All the rats I know are holed up until spring. This granary is a good place—food, water, shelter. Why not stay here?"

Frederick wasn't taking any chances on explaining their mission to another stranger. "Take my word for it. We have to go, and soon."

"Such a pity you don't have wings." Edgar examined the rats—first with one eye, then the other. "But since you can't fly, why not take the train? Swiss trains are the best in the world. They run like clockwork. In fact, the train you'd want runs very near here. I've flown over it many a time. A red train called the Glacier Express."

"Perfect!" said Frederick. "We can jump on when it stops at the village station."

"Doesn't stop here," said the raven. "It only slows down to go around a bend in the track before entering the tunnel."

"There's got to be some way we can get on that train," Frederick said.

Edgar scratched under his wing with his foot. "Sounds bird-brained to me—rats traveling to Zermatt. Still, if you absolutely must go, I have an idea. I could fly over the train as it slows and drop you on the roof."

"Drop us?" Ishbu stared at Edgar's talons. "You mean snatch us up in your claws, fly into the storm, and drop us onto the slippery and narrow roof of a speeding train?"

Edgar nodded. "That's it!" he crowed. "Precisely."

Ishbu turned pale. He shook his head stubbornly. "No! If we miss the roof of the train, we'll be smashed on the rocks! Even if we manage to land on the roof, we might still end up smashed on the rocks!"

Frederick chewed his toenails, considering. He knew that seagulls dropped shells from great heights in order to crack them open on rocks and eat the tender insides. He thought of his own tender insides. Could they trust the raven not to smash them intentionally?

In the end, after a hasty discussion, Frederick and Ishbu agreed to let Edgar drop them onto the train. "What choice do we have?" Frederick said.

Ishbu frowned at his brother. If it were up to him, he'd choose Miss Dove's cage!

They waited in the chilly granary until Edgar cocked his head. "Best be getting on," he said. "I hear the train whistle."

The rats heard it, too—low and mournful. The raven carefully picked up each rat by the scruff of the neck.

"Oof," he said to Ishbu. "What have you been eating?"

Ishbu made a face.

The bird took off, gaining altitude by circling

above the granary. It was still snowing steadily, but the wind had died down. Frederick and Ishbu dangled from Edgar's talons. Ishbu shut his eyes, but Frederick found this an amazing way to travel. His neck hurt a bit where the talons slightly pierced his skin, but really, it wasn't much different from when he was a baby and his mother used to pick him up with her teeth.

And the view! Beneath his paws, Frederick saw snowy fields, the granary, the roofs of the village chalets, and the train tracks. It looked like a model set with a pocket-size red locomotive rumbling along, trailing a plume of white from the smokestack.

Edgar soared over the train. "I'm going to get as near as I can," he panted. "The roof might be wet. Try not to slide off!" With that, he swooped down, opened his talons . . . and let go.

A FUR-RAISING RIDE

THE TWO RATS WHIRLED THROUGH the air, Ishbu shrieking and Frederick calling, "Thanks!" They landed paws down on top of the train. Ishbu lost his balance and skidded toward the edge. Frederick caught him by the tail and yanked him to safety.

Or relative safety. Even though Edgar had said the train would slow down, it still felt incredibly fast to the two rats. Trees and rocks and cliffs whizzed past. The Glacier Express gave a whistle like a scream and roared into the tunnel.

There was complete and utter darkness, the only sound the wheels screeching on the track, then—whoosh!—out into the mountains. The train crossed stone bridges above snow-filled ravines, snaked around tight curves, and plunged into valleys alongside frozen streams. The blowing snow pelted them like hail.

Ishbu's stomach rolled, and he turned a familiar shade of green.

"Hold on!" shouted Frederick. The words were snatched out of his mouth. Somehow, the two rats found paw holds on the metal surface of the train's roof and clung like barnacles. The wind pinned their ears back and blew their whiskers askew. Their paws, tails, and ears grew numb.

After what felt like hours, the train slowed and jerked as the track changed to a cogwheel system —like the uphill part of a roller coaster. They began the climb into the higher elevations of the Alps.

Ishbu squeezed his eyes shut—opening them once, briefly, to see an ibex (a type of mountain goat) staring at them from a rocky ledge. The ibex snorted as if to say, "I've seen everything now!" Then in a blink, they'd passed him by, climbing straight into the clouds, the train clinging to the edge of the cliff. Frederick peeked cautiously over the side and glimpsed a ravine filled with jagged rocks.

With a wail of its whistle, the train plunged down into the valley.

Just when they thought they couldn't hold on to the roof one second longer, the train shuddered and slowed again. A few scattered chalets appeared, and then more, clustered close together as the train click-clacked through town. They stopped in the shelter of the village station in a burst of steam.

"Zermatt!" the conductor announced over the loudspeaker.

Trembling from head to tail, the rat brothers crawled to the side of the roof and slid down to the platform.

They took cover beneath a baggage cart. Ishbu's stomach churned. "Ooh, Freddy," he moaned. "I'm going to be sick." And he was. Frederick patted his brother's back, took a breath of the thin mountain air, and looked around. The station was packed with tourists pushing baggage carts loaded with skis, knapsacks, and luggage. A group of schoolchildren crowded around their teacher, and Frederick was suddenly homesick for Miss Dove and Wilberforce Harrison Elementary School.

But we've done it, thought Frederick, brushing snowflakes off Ishbu's fur. Even without the help of the Swiss A.B.O.B., they'd reached Zermatt. *Now what?*

SIGNED, SEALED, DELIVERED

THE RATS WANDERED THROUGH the station, confused, tired, and hungry. Ishbu found a morsel of bratwurst and began to nibble.

"How can you eat so soon after being sick?" asked Frederick, sharing the sausage.

Ishbu shrugged and went on eating. "What can I say? I'm a rat!"

The two rats lapped melted snow from the gutter. Then they continued through the crowded station —Frederick searching for any clue that might lead them to the factory, Ishbu searching for more snacks.

Frederick found nothing. Not a trace, not a track, not an inkling. Nothing that might guide them to the Big Cheese, the pet food factory, or Natasha. The rats huddled inside under a bench. A steady draft whistled through the open doors. Frederick slumped down, his whiskers drooping.

"If only we had something to go on," Frederick said. "If only we could find the factory, or the members of the Swiss A.B.O.B. They could help. But where do we look for badgers? The forests? The mountains? There must be thirty mountain peaks near Zermatt! It will take forever! And every minute counts." He dropped his head into his paws again.

Ishbu tried to cheer up his brother by offering a piece of croissant he'd found in the gutter. "Too bad we can't just mail ourselves to the factory," he joked.

Frederick couldn't help but laugh at the image. "In a package. Addressed to 'Mr. Big Cheese, Tasty Tails Pet Food Company, Zermatt, Switzerland.'" Then he sat up straight. "Ishbu," he said, "I think you've got something!"

Ishbu wrinkled his nose. "Mail ourselves? I was just kidding!"

Frederick began to pace. "I know. But listen. The factory must get mail. In fact, they must get regular deliveries—ingredients for pet food, printed labels, empty cans . . . all sorts of stuff."

Ishbu scratched behind his ears and waited for Frederick to go on. He still didn't get it.

"They must receive some deliveries by train, and the deliveries come in boxes, I bet. Cardboard boxes. Addressed to the factory." Frederick's whiskers curled up. "If we could find where the boxes get picked up, crawl in, and—"

Ishbu jumped up and hugged his brother. "And presto! We're on our way right to the factory door!"

It didn't turn out to be quite that easy. The train station in Zermatt wasn't very big, but it was very busy. The rats scuttled through the crowds along the platform, in and out of rooms and alcoves: lost luggage, passenger pick up and drop off, ticket counters, banking counters, food counters, and telephone booths. Meanwhile, on the rails beside them, wheels screeched as the trains arrived and departed.

Frederick led the way between sightseers, skiers, police officers, couples, singles, newlyweds, and families with children. The rats were cautious, and, to their relief, everyone seemed too busy to notice them. After a while, poor Ishbu's tail was dragging, but Frederick urged him on.

At last they found the baggage claim area, a room piled high with bundles waiting to be picked up, bulky things too big for the passenger railcars: large trunks and suitcases, snowboards, sleds, skis, and strollers. In the corner were several stacks of cardboard boxes.

"This might be what we're looking for!" Frederick cried. He eagerly began reading address labels. Ishbu helped by snuffling the boxes that smelled like food.

Frederick found packages addressed to hotels, shops, restaurants, private chalets, the hospital, and post office boxes. Then he found a stack of cartons three feet high addressed in red: *Tasty Tails Pet Food Company.*

Frederick grinned at Ishbu. "This is it!" he said.

"What do we do now?" asked Ishbu.

"We hide. And wait to be picked up."

Frederick gnawed a U-shaped flap in the side of one of the boxes. They climbed in, and he lowered the flap to conceal them.

Unfortunately for Ishbu, the box wasn't filled with pet food ingredients. It was filled with empty cans. "I hope we don't have to wait forever," said Ishbu. "I forgot to pack snacks."

The rats waited so long, they fell asleep. They awoke to movement. Frederick lifted the flap and saw that their box had been loaded with others onto a handcart and was now being trundled through the station. The rats' boxes were taken outside, where they were packed into the rear of an electric van.

The rats bounced around as the van drove over the cobblestone streets. Frederick lifted the flap again so he could look out the back window.

A break in the clouds allowed the sunlight to sparkle on the snow-frosted chalets and, above them, Frederick saw the Matterhorn! The famous mountain towered over the village, imposing and dangerous. Frederick wondered how many climbers had tried to scale it and failed.

The delivery van stopped a couple of times, dropping off packages. Whenever they stopped, Frederick slid back inside the box so he wouldn't be seen.

Eventually, the Tasty Tails boxes were the only ones left. The van pulled up to a station with an empty cable car sitting in front. Frederick and Ishbu were familiar with the San Francisco cable cars that run on a cable embedded in the street. But these Swiss cable cars ran on steel wires suspended far above the ground. Frederick knew they were called gondolas. He thought the red cars looked like boxes of animal crackers on strings—carrying humans up and down the mountains to the ski lifts and bobsled runs.

This particular station was clearly a private operation. Frederick examined the sign above the entrance. It was written in all the languages of Switzerland: German, French, Italian, and English. Although he could read only the English, the warning was all too clear.

PRIVATE. NO TRESPASSING!
PRIVE. DEFENSE D'ENTRER!
PRIVAT. BETRETEN VERBOTEN!
RISERVATO. VIETATO L'ACCESSO!

Frederick popped back inside the box as the delivery man unloaded the Tasty Tails cartons and stacked them on the handcart. He showed his pass at the gate, greeting the operator. It sounded like German, but Frederick didn't know what they said. *Oh, to be multilingual like Professor Ratinsky!* The delivery man pushed the handcart on board the gondola, and the door hissed closed.

Frederick poked his nose out again. After all, he might never get another chance to ride in a gondola. The car jerked once and swayed as it was pulled above the ground on the strong steel lines. Overhead, the cables glistened against the evening sky. Frederick was amazed to see the trees and rocks dropping farther and farther away. Inside the box, Ishbu curled up in a ball and put his tail over his eyes.

The ride didn't take long. With a final lurch, the gondola docked at a station on the top of the mountain slope.

THE SHADOW OF
THE MATTERHORN

A FEW MINUTES LATER, THE brothers crouched behind a boulder overlooking a road. They were above the tree line now, a grim landscape composed of snow, rocks, and bare mountain peaks. The curved fang of the Matterhorn rose nearby.

Frederick and Ishbu had snuck out of the box as soon as the delivery man pushed the handcart out of the gondola. Now they hid and watched to see where he went.

The snow had been plowed into piles on either side of the road. The banks were so high that the road was almost a tunnel. The delivery man walked along, pushing his cart, his footsteps muffled by the snow.

Where's he going? wondered Frederick. This couldn't be the factory. There were no buildings, no smokestacks, no machinery. It looked as if the road simply ended at a rockslide.

After everything it took to get to here, had they reached a dead end? They watched the man unload his cart, leaving the boxes stacked in front of the rocks. Then he walked back to the cable car station.

"Let's investigate," said Frederick. "But be careful. Something's funny about this whole thing."

The two rats crept from their hiding place, slid down the snowbank, and scurried up the road. Boxes. Rocks. Snow. There was nothing else to see, but rats don't rely on sight alone. Frederick nosed the rocks, and his whiskers twitched.

He could have sworn he smelled cinnamon. "*Natasha!*" he whispered. Ishbu regarded him curiously. "She's close. I know it," Frederick said. He slid his paws across the rocks. *Aha!* Between two rocks there was a metal door, cleverly painted to blend in with the boulders!

But the door was sealed shut. Not a crack, not a gap, not a crevice. No space wide enough for a whisker, let alone an entire rat.

"This *must* be it," muttered Frederick. "Who else would build a door here? And disguise it."

Ishbu didn't have to ask who Frederick was talking about. He sucked his tail as Frederick scratched the door. It pinged softly as his claws hit the painted metal.

"How will we get inside? Maybe we should just get back into the box and wait for someone to bring us in," said Ishbu.

Frederick pinged the door again thoughtfully. "And risk getting caught by whoever's inside? No, let's find our own way in there."

Factory, fortress, hideout, or headquarters, Frederick knew any animals inside would need air to breathe. "Sniff, Ishbu. Use your nose! There must be an air vent or duct or shaft. And where there are holes, rats can enter!"

They found a vent at last, hidden behind a rock outcropping. One at a time, the rats wriggled through and followed the duct inside the mountain. It was a tight squeeze for Ishbu, but he felt much safer in the enclosed, dark space.

Frederick held his ears high, and his nose was alert to danger. He noted other ducts branching off that might afford escape routes should they be trapped. But despite his caution, he ran rapidly, thinking of Natasha somewhere ahead, somewhere close. He knew it!

The main duct ended abruptly at a wire grill. Frederick and Ishbu crouched behind it, gazing down on an open room filled with gleaming machinery. A conveyor belt crossed the center of the room, traveling past vats and pipes, valves, gauges, and sensors. And along the belt, cans of food . . . Frederick couldn't see inside them, but the smell was overpowering—lamb, fish, chicken, beef, grain.

Ishbu's tummy growled.

"I have to get closer," Frederick murmured. "Stay here. I'm going down."

"No!" said Ishbu, grabbing his brother's tail. "It's too risky."

"I'm counting on you to be my backup," Frederick said. "If something happens to me . . ."

Ishbu's eyes glistened, but he didn't say anything. He let Frederick's tail slide through his paws. He helped gnaw a hole in the wire grate, and Frederick wiggled through, dropping softly to the floor. Ishbu watched Frederick creep along the wall and round the corner before moving out of view.

"Be careful, Freddy," Ishbu whispered, and then he sat down in the dusty vent alone.

TASTY TAILS

FREDERICK SCUTTLED ALONG, keeping close to the wall. The concrete floor of the processing room was covered with rubber matting. Open doors hinted at hallways beyond.

He saw no workers—neither human nor animal—and he realized that the factory was automated. Chimes and whistles sounded from time to time. Huge stainless steel vats sent up clouds of odorous steam. Open cans whizzed past on the long conveyor belt. Machines hissed, groaned, blitzed, and whirred. Brown chunks of meat plopped into each can, followed by a squirt of gravy. More whirring and creaking and hissing, as the cans were sealed and sent along the line.

Frederick edged closer. He recognized the red and yellow labels of the Tasty Tails Pet Food Company on the cans and the slogan: "Mouthwatering Meals for

Perfect Pets." He swallowed hard. The smell was everywhere. Frederick had a nearly unbearable longing to scramble up the conveyor belt and gobble some food. But who knew what was really in those cans?

As he studied the production line, a howl cut through the whine of machinery and then changed to sobbing.

Natasha! What was happening to her? Frederick followed his ears, darting through an open door and into a passage. Suddenly, he found his path blocked by a familiar face.

Beady pink eyes, tulip-shaped ears, a champagne coat—Mo-Mo!

The mouse smiled. "I bet you're surprised to see me."

"Out of my way!" shouted Frederick. "I've got to find her."

Mo-Mo snickered. "Too late, old chap. We found you first."

He turned and whistled over his shoulder. Snip and Snarl charged down the hall.

"It's time to greet the Big Cheese," Snarl growled.

ISHBU'S ADVENTURE

 ISHBU SAT IN THE VENT, SUCKING his tail and trying not to sneeze. The howl, when it came, made his fur stand on end.

Was it Freddy? What should he do? Should he follow?

But the wail didn't seem to come from the processing room below. It sounded farther away. Maybe the air duct led to another room. With his ears perked, Ishbu loped back through the vent to the next branching.

This vent also ended in a wire grill. The howl had stopped, but Ishbu heard voices. He inched closer and peeked through the grill into a room. No furniture, no rugs, only concrete walls and floor, as bleak and bare as a prison cell. A single bulb hung from the ceiling, spotlighting the scene, leaving the corners of the room murky with shadows.

Under the harsh light, a couple of weasels gripped

a lilac rat. Ishbu's heart skipped a beat. Then he realized it wasn't his brother. It was—

Natasha!

Ishbu squeaked. He quickly covered his mouth and hunkered down, snout pressed to the wire, eyes wide.

He saw that beside Natasha and the weasels, two hulking ferrets stood over an old, gray rat tied to a chair. A pair of broken spectacles perched on the rat's snout. Professor Ratinsky!

The ferrets were talking. Ishbu strained to hear.

"This is your last chance. No more stalling. You know what the Big Cheese wants," demanded the larger ferret, shaking his paw in front of the professor's snout. "Give us the formula!"

"Never," said the professor hoarsely. The ferret kicked him, and the old rat groaned. Natasha struggled against the weasels holding her, but they yanked her back.

The other ferret snorted. "You'll change your tune when we put your daughter in this again!" He gestured toward the corner.

For the first time, Ishbu saw what lurked in the shadows like a living creature. *A rat trap!* A chill like ice water ran down his spine as he imagined the wicked crack of the spring, the force of the bar snapping down.

"Do not be giving in, Papa!" cried Natasha. "It

matters not what happens to me!"

Professor Ratinsky attempted a weak smile. "Not to worry, my little Natka. Big Cheese will never get formula."

The weasels began to drag Natasha toward the trap.

Tears sprang to Ishbu's eyes. He hadn't realized Natasha could be so selfless and so brave. He knew it was no use—he couldn't fight four hench-beasts on his own; but he couldn't sit here and let this happen. He scrabbled at the wire grill covering the vent, trying to get in.

At the sound, the ferrets turned their cold eyes up toward him. . . .

IN THE HALL OF
THE MOUNTAIN KING

 FREDERICK DANGLED HELPLESSLY FROM Snip's powerful jaws as the two rat terriers and the show mouse ran down a hall to a steel door. Mo-Mo turned a tiny gold key in the lock on the wall, and a panel slid open. The animals stepped inside a cagelike room.

Frederick had never been in an elevator before. He felt a moment of claustrophobia as the door swept shut. Mo-Mo punched the button labeled Penthouse. An arrow on a dial above the door flicked to the right as they passed floor after floor. Frederick's tummy dropped, and the door hissed open.

Snip tossed Frederick to the floor. He landed on his back on a plush carpet. He stood, a bit wobbly, wiped off the terrier's saliva, and stared in astonishment.

The view was stunning. They must have ridden the elevator through the core of the mountain to the very top. Three walls of the penthouse were composed of floor-to-ceiling windows. The icy peak of the Matterhorn filled one of the windows, and through the others, Frederick saw distant snow-capped peaks, blushing pink in the alpenglow. Down in the valley, the lights of Zermatt sparkled like fireflies as the evening sky turned violet.

Bookcases, filing cabinets, and an immense desk were set against the windowless wall. Above the desk, a cuckoo clock chirped the hour. And next to it, hanging from a hook—Professor Ratinsky's medal! The gold glinted in the last rays of sunlight.

A cough caught Frederick's attention, and he swiveled around. Seated in a high-backed leather chair, clutching his white-tipped cane, was the Big Cheese.

"What an unexpected pleasure, Mr. Frederick."

"Not for me," Frederick said hotly. "Where's Natasha? Where's Professor Ratinsky? What have you done with them?"

The albino opossum sneered, showing all fifty teeth, and turned to his hench-beasts. "Snip, stay here. Mo-Mo, Snarl, go find the other intruder. They seem to travel in pairs."

He waved his paw in Frederick's direction. "You'll see the girl soon enough. But before you do, tell me what you think of my new headquarters. I hear the view is spectacular. An engineering marvel beyond compare, built inside the mountain itself. You know the Swiss built more than one hundred of these secret fortresses during World War II? Hollowed out of solid rock." He didn't wait for Frederick to comment. "By gad, sir, it is the ideal setting for my ideal crime."

"Ideal crime?" said Frederick scornfully. "Making pet food? Or do you mean the jewel thefts?"

"Ah, yes," said the possum, "the thefts. Nothing more than a little creative financing to fund my operation. Pet food factories, hideouts in the Swiss Alps, private gondolas—they don't come cheap, I can assure you. But the burglaries are trifles compared to my brilliant scheme."

"What scheme?" asked Frederick.

The Big Cheese folded his paws across his enormous stomach. "There are none as blind as those who cannot see," he said in his throaty purr. "My dear fellow, my sole aim in life is to rid the world of those creatures who clog our air and waterways, who litter the forests and spoil our deserts, oceans, and mountains. The only species that wages war; the only species that soils its own nest. Do I make myself clear?"

Frederick knew the Big Cheese needed no answer, and the possum didn't wait for one. "Why, humans, of course!" he continued, smiling. "And what is the only species that keeps pets? That enslaves domestic animals to do their bidding? Again, humans! Imagine how surprised they will be when their dear cats and dogs rise up and kill their masters!"

"But how? I don't understand." Frederick leaned forward. If he could keep the Big Cheese talking, he might find out something useful.

"Really, Mr. Frederick. I expected better of you. Never mind. I will explain. I am on the verge of creating a pet food with a special ingredient—a secret ingredient, if you will. Soon cats and dogs will obey me, and at my signal, they will rid the world of those blasted humans, making it safe for animals. Of course, animals will need a new master," he said with a smirk. "And I will be happy to oblige!"

Kill all humans! Frederick instantly thought of Miss Dove, her soft voice and gentle hands, the corsage of violets she often wore on her sweater, her stories and lessons. And what about the schoolchildren—playing dodge ball on the playground, offering tidbits of leftover lunches through the cage bars, Barnaby and Kitty unknowingly teaching him to read. . . .

"You beast!" Frederick cried. "But how did you develop this pet food? Professor Ratinsky— don't tell me he's helping you!"

The possum narrowed his blind eyes. "When my spies told me about the professor's formula, I ordered my scientists to devise a similar compound. They failed," the possum admitted. "The animals that eat it are hypnotized but won't obey me. So I brought the professor here to assist us. His formula is the last piece of the puzzle. So far he has refused to give it to me." The Big Cheese tightened his grip on his cane. "But he will. I'm sure his daughter will persuade him. And now you can help. I know you won't want to see anything unfortunate happen to the girl rat or to your—"

The elevator doors slid open again, and Snarl and Mo-Mo entered. Snarl dragged Ishbu by the neck. He flung him in front of the Big Cheese. "The ferrets found him in the air shaft," he gloated. "How's about I finish him off, boss?"

"When I give the order," said the Big Cheese. His milky eyes glowed like opals.

Ishbu limped over to Frederick. One of his paws was bleeding. Frederick put his arm around his brother and turned to the Big Cheese. "You will never succeed, because Natasha and the professor are too good to fall in with your schemes."

"So far," said the possum, "I have put up with your annoyances because I respect your intelligence. But my patience is wearing thin."

A mangy weasel stepped off the elevator. "Inspector Magnus," she said, saluting smartly. "Making my report, sir."

"Now?" the Big Cheese snapped. "Can't you see I'm occupied?"

The weasel rubbed her paws together. "Begging

your pardon, sir, it can't wait. The Number Ten filter is broken again. Dust is building up. We'll have to shut down production until we get the filter running, or else—"

"Pah!" The Big Cheese stood up. "Must I take care of everything myself?"

He leaned over Frederick and Ishbu, and his breath was sour in Frederick's face. "It would be a pity to have to exterminate such a worthy adversary as yourself, Mr. Frederick. I can use a resourceful rat like you in my organization. Here is what I propose: join me, and after the professor gives me his formula, I will let your friends go. Refuse, and you all die. What do you say?"

For the tiniest moment, Frederick wavered. It was a terrifying offer, but it would be a small price to pay for the others' safety. . . .

"No, Freddy!" cried Ishbu. "Remember the A.B.O.B.! 'Never give up, never let go'!"

Frederick came back to his senses. *Good old Ishbu! I can always trust him to point the way.* He curled his paws into fists and glared at his enemy. "Never."

"Lock them up!" thundered the Big Cheese.

LAB RATS

THE TERRIERS DRAGGED FREDERICK AND Ishbu back into the elevator. Mo-Mo used his gold key. He hit the down button, and the rats' tummies rose as the elevator dropped. When the door slid open, they were in a tunnel in the very bowels of the mountain.

The air was bitterly cold and smelled stale. The dogs, with the rats pinched between their teeth, trotted through a tunnel lit only by bare bulbs dangling from the ceiling.

The tunnel ended at a steel door, which Mo-Mo unlocked. The dogs spit the rats into the room. The door slammed shut with an echoing clang. Frederick heard the click of the lock and the footsteps of the retreating animals.

Ishbu groaned and began to lick his wounded paw. Frederick sat up painfully, rubbing his neck where Snarl's teeth had pierced his skin.

The room was pitch-black. A hot tear slid down Frederick's nose. He licked it away. He mustn't give in to self-pity.

"Frederick? Is that you?" A whisper, faint but with an unmistakable Russian accent . . .

The scratch of a match, a whiff of sulfur—and in the soft glow—Natasha!

She was thinner than when Frederick had last seen her. Her lovely coat was grimy with dust. Her black eyes filled with tears when she saw him.

"You came!" she cried, running to him. Frederick bent his head and brushed the top of hers lightly with his whiskers. He caught the trace of cinnamon on her fur. "I left message in dungeon, praying that you live, and here you are."

"You must be Frederick," said a voice behind him, "and Ishbu." Frederick turned, his paw still around Natasha, and saw an elderly rat holding a Bunsen burner aloft like a lamp.

"Allow me please to introduce my father, Professor Ratinsky," said Natasha.

Frederick politely sniffed the old rat. The professor smelled of chemicals—sulfur, acid, iodine. The fur on his muzzle was white. A pair of spectacles rested on his nose, slightly askew. The bridge had been broken and the glasses taped together. He looked frail, and Frederick could see that imprisonment had taken a toll on the old rat.

Ishbu came over and clicked his teeth at the others. The four of them quickly caught up on the events that brought them to the factory.

"We owe much to you, Ishbu," said Natasha. "You distracted weasels from using rat trap on me."

Ishbu's ears turned pink at her praise. Then he sighed. "It didn't do much good, though. They'll just try again tomorrow."

"Tomorrow is a whole day away," said Frederick as he began to examine the room. "Maybe we'll have figured something out by then."

The light from the Bunsen burner shone on a wooden table covered with test tubes, flasks, jars of colored liquids and powders. Scattered across the top of the workbench were papers, books, slide rules, pencils, and pens.

"It's a laboratory!" said Frederick.

Professor Ratinsky nodded. "Big Cheese built it. That I might create this." He held out a folded paper packet, the kind that chemists use to keep powders dry.

"The secret ingredient! You made it, then?" Frederick asked.

"*Da,*" said the professor. "Once here I am curious; I cannot keep from experiments to pass time. To see if I can remember without my notes." He tapped his head. "But I have not anyone to try it out on. Perhaps it does not work."

The professor's face became serious. "Big Cheese will never have for evil deeds!" Despite his weak appearance, his voice rang with determination. "I keep this hidden, always." He slid the packet carefully between the pages of a chemistry book on his workbench.

Frederick wondered if it was really safe in the book—but he didn't argue. Instead, he continued his exploration, rubbing his paws across the rock walls, tapping them, looking for exits.

"There must be some way out of here," he said.

"Impossible," Professor Ratinsky replied. "When first I came, I tried . . . until I grew too ill. We are underground. This room is carved out of mountain itself—solid granite. Only one door, which is locked, as you see."

"How about air vents?" asked Frederick.

The professor pointed at the ceiling. Frederick climbed on the workbench and lunged at the vent, but it was much too far away for a rat to reach.

"Even if we could get out of room, only way to leave factory is metal door at front—always guarded, I am sure—or through windows in penthouse," Professor Ratinsky added.

"But isn't the Big Cheese always there?" asked Natasha. "Every time I'm taken to see him, he's waiting—like hideous monster in lair."

"*Da*, he leaves only to inspect factory," said the professor. "Every morning he does so. He used to be making me go with him until I am getting sick."

"Then we must get into his office when he's gone," said Frederick.

"But how?" asked Ishbu.

It seemed there was no answer. They talked for hours, inventing plans, then dismissing them. Frederick sat chewing his toenails. Every now and then, someone would leap up and say, "How about . . . ?" But each plan ended in failure. It was hopeless.

Ishbu yawned and rubbed his empty belly. Natasha's long, elegant whiskers drooped. The Professor looked exhausted.

"Let's get some rest," said Frederick. "Maybe we'll think of something in the morning." He didn't add that time might be running out.

The rats began to groom before settling down to sleep.

"There's something I've been wondering about, Professor," said Frederick as he washed his paws. "Why did you create your formula in the first place?"

The professor scrubbed his ears thoughtfully. "I never intended to hypnotize animals," he said. "It is side result of my experiments on animal-human communication. Same research for which I am awarded Benevolence Medal."

"The Big Cheese has your medal," Frederick said. "I saw it in his office. I wonder why he keeps it. Seems like he'd sell it."

No one answered, but as Frederick cleaned his whiskers, he thought perhaps the Big Cheese might envy the professor. *The Big Cheese can never be the good guy. He'll never win awards and honors and respect. Maybe he keeps the medal because he's jealous.*

The Professor turned off the flame on the Bunsen burner to save fuel, plunging the room into darkness. With the light gone, the cold seemed more intense. The four rats curled up together on the stone floor to stay warm.

Frederick felt Natasha's whiskers brush his. "Are you really all right?" he asked. "I found bloodstains in the dungeon."

"Just a scratch," said Natasha.

"I found your nail file, too," he told her, "but I must have lost it somewhere on the journey."

"It matters not," she said. "You are here."

Frederick smiled. Even though they were locked in a secret laboratory beneath a mountain in the Swiss Alps, he was glad to be with Natasha again. He couldn't let her down.

But how could he rescue them all?

ISHBU PERFORMS

THE RATS SLEPT SOUNDLY. THE room remained as black as night. Only the rattle of a key in the lock and the creak of the door told them it was morning.

Frederick staggered to his feet. He rubbed the sleep from his eyes and peered at the door.

Mo-Mo stood there, sleek and well groomed as always, carrying a battery-powered lantern in one paw and a covered dish in the other. A linen napkin was draped over his arm. "Breakfast for the famous scientist," he said breezily. "Wouldn't do to let him starve, now would it?"

He set the lantern on the floor, put the dish on the workbench, and whisked off the cover. Pet food—*Tasty Tails* pet food. The smell wafted under Frederick's nose, making him drool.

The professor waved his wrinkled paw. "*Nyet.* Take

it away," he said. "I will not eat until you release my daughter."

Mo-Mo flourished the napkin. "Come now, Professor. How will that help your daughter? All you have to do to save her is to give the boss the formula. It's simple, if I do say so myself."

"You betrayed our friendship!" cried Natasha with a defiant tilt of her head. "We will never be giving in!"

"We'll see about that," said Mo-Mo. "As soon as the boss gets done with inspection, he's planned another little session with the rat trap. Since you were so rudely interrupted yesterday." Mo-Mo scowled at Ishbu and then turned back to Natasha and her father.

While Mo-Mo argued with the professor over the food, Frederick edged toward the professor's workbench.

"A diversion, Ishbu," he whispered, sniffing the plate of food. "Create a diversion."

"A *what*?" asked Ishbu.

"Distract him!" Frederick hissed. "Make him look at *you*!"

Ishbu's eyes widened. "What am I supposed to do? Tap dance?" he whispered. Then he laughed out loud. "Hey, everybody!" he called. "Want to see what I can do?"

He began to hum and pound his feet. Natasha and the professor stared at him, confused. Frederick recognized the Highland Badger Fling. He was amazed that Ishbu remembered it.

Mo-Mo glared at Ishbu impatiently. He didn't see Frederick pull the white packet from between the pages of the book and sprinkle the powder across the dish of pet food. The powder dissolved instantly.

"You cut that out," Mo-Mo told Ishbu. "No dancing. Absolutely not!"

But Ishbu didn't stop. He hummed and whirled in time to his drumming paws. He added a kick and a clever little step as he sang the A.B.O.B. anthem. "*Tyrants fall in every foe,*" he trumpeted. "*Liberty's in every blow! Let us do or die!*"

"You'll sing a different tune when the Big Cheese gets done with you," snapped Mo-Mo. He swung back to address the others. "Eat your breakfast, Professor. It smells scrumptious."

The professor shook his head. "Not until Natasha is freed."

Mo-Mo looked worried. "I'm not going to take this food back to the Big Cheese and tell him I failed again." Then his eyes twinkled. "Well," he said, "what he doesn't know won't hurt him. If you aren't going to eat it . . ."

And Mo-Mo gobbled the pet food right down. "Excellent!" he said, dabbing his whiskers with the napkin.

Frederick held his breath and watched.

Slowly Mo-Mo's eyes rolled back in his head. He stood completely still, as though listening to a voice only he could hear, just like the black cat in the German farmyard.

"I slipped the powder into his food," Frederick whispered to the others. "Let's see if it works." He faced the blank-eyed mouse. "Take us to the penthouse!" he ordered.

For a moment, Mo-Mo didn't move. Then he pivoted as though executing a military turn and marched to the door.

Mo-Mo unlocked the dungeon door, and the rats followed him out of the laboratory and down the passage to the elevator. Without a word, Mo-Mo opened the elevator with his key and pushed the Penthouse button. At the top floor, the rats stole cautiously into the Big Cheese's office. It was empty.

"He'll be back soon," said Professor Ratinsky. "We don't have much time."

"What should we do with *him*?" asked Natasha, gesturing to Mo-Mo. He stood at the open elevator door, smiling vacantly.

The rats regarded him thoughtfully. Then Ishbu spoke up. "I've got an idea," he said. "Something I learned from the fifth graders." He pointed at the mouse. "Go pull the fire alarm," he ordered. Mo-Mo marched back into the elevator. The door closed.

"Good thinking!" said Frederick. "That will keep

everyone busy for a while. No one will use the elevator in case it's a real fire. And your Highland Badger Fling—Ishbu! It was inspired!"

Ishbu blushed with pleasure.

"Now on to our escape!" Frederick said, rubbing his paws.

LESSONS FROM HISTORY

IF ONLY THE RATS HADN'T BEEN LOCKED up all night underground, away from doors and windows—if only they had seen the ring around the moon, Frederick might have remembered Miss Dove saying, "Halo around the sun or moon, rain or snow is coming soon." If only they could have seen the village of Zermatt, they might have noticed how the smoke from the chimneys curled downward and lingered near the ground—a sure sign of an approaching storm.

If they knew that the ibexes had migrated down from the mountains and the hares had taken to open ground, maybe they would have realized that a big storm—a *very* big storm—was on the way.

But even now, glancing out a window, Frederick was too distracted to note the threatening blue-black clouds.

Ishbu stood next to his brother, gazing down at the snowdrifts far below. "Even if we could get out of here, we'd never be able to climb all the way down the mountain," he warned.

"We can't stay here," said Frederick. The four rats shoved the window open. A few fragile snowflakes swirled inside and melted on the carpet. "We'll have to take our chances."

"I follow you, my friend." Professor Ratinsky stretched out his thin paws. "I would rather die free than be forced to work for madman."

"I go with you," said Natasha.

"Count me in, too, Freddy," said Ishbu. But his whiskers trembled.

As glad as Frederick was to hear this, the responsibility to see all four of them to safety weighed on him.

"Here's what we'll do," he said. "We'll climb out the window and try to lower ourselves down. Maybe we can find a rope or something. Then we'll hike down the mountain."

"And leave trail?" Natasha asked. "We will be making tracks in snow. So easy for Bilgewater Brigade to follow!"

"We wouldn't leave tracks if we could fly," Ishbu said, remembering the raven.

"Fly," murmured Frederick. His eyes lit up. "We can't fly, but we *can* glide!"

"Watch!" Frederick grabbed a scrap of paper from the desk and began to fold. Soon he had a paper airplane. The fifth graders made paper airplanes like this and held contests to see which glided the farthest.

"Look!" Frederick cried, giving it a toss. The plane sped toward the ceiling, looped once, and then drifted down to the floor. "We'll glide straight down the mountain to the village. From there we can take the train to safety."

Ishbu picked up the paper airplane. "Nice try, Freddy, but this is too light to hold us. And it didn't go very far. And what about steering?"

Frederick's shoulders slumped.

"Wait," said Professor Ratinsky. "Young rat may be on to something. If we build glider from heavier paper . . . maybe file folder? And if we have way to launch it—"

"Like a catapult!" shouted Frederick. Ideas were now coming as thick and fast as the snowflakes outside. "Medieval armies used catapults to launch boulders over castle walls. We could build a catapult to launch the glider. Make the plane sturdy enough so it will hold all of us. Calculate the angle of trajectory, the velocity, air drag, lift . . ."

"Now that's something I can be helping with," said the professor, stroking his whiskers. He began jotting down figures with a pencil from the Big Cheese's desk.

"I can fold!" said Natasha. "I will be making glider."

"I'll help," said Ishbu.

Natasha and Ishbu scrambled up the desk to a pile of file folders. They pulled one free and dumped out the contents, sending papers cascading across the floor. The two rats sat on the desk and began to crease the manila folder, using their teeth to flatten the folds. Frederick watched them happily. It seemed Ishbu had finally forgiven Natasha.

"A catapult . . . ," Frederick said, surveying the room. "What can we use? We need a source of energy." He spotted a cardboard box in the corner. Stenciled across the front were big red letters: RAT TRAPS. His fur rose at the sight, but he bravely opened the box and dragged out one of the traps.

"Don't mess with that!" Ishbu called out.

"We can use this to make our catapult!" replied Frederick. He explained his idea to Professor Ratinsky.

"Ah, I am seeing what you mean," said the professor, looking up from his notes. He settled his spectacles more firmly on his nose. "First, let us build ramp from books, no? I will determine proper angle. We don't want to hit wall instead of going out window!"

The rats pulled a few volumes from the bookshelves and piled them into a ramp, using

Professor Ratinsky's figures. Together, they dragged the trap to the top.

Frederick pried open the bar.

"Careful!" cried Natasha as it snapped back with a sharp crack.

"Whew, that was close," Frederick said, sucking his sore paw. "It will take all of us to pull it down. We'd better lash it in place."

They dug through the desk drawers until they found a thick piece of twine. With a great deal of grunting, the four rats managed to secure the deadly bar.

"But what's to stop it from flinging our plane to the ground and snapping on us?" asked Ishbu.

Frederick pulled a ruler and a couple of erasers out of a pencil cup. Using tape he found on the desk, he fastened the ruler to the bar of the rat trap. "This will be the throwing arm," he said as he worked. "We'll attach the glider to this." When he finished, he stacked the erasers against the spring of the trap. "If we tape the erasers here, they should stop the bar at the top of its arc. The force will throw us clear of the trap. If we figured the angle correctly, we'll fly out the window." He looked at the professor. "Do you think it'll work?"

Professor Ratinsky nodded. "We find out."

The sound of the fire alarm blared through the room. Mo-Mo had completed his orders.

"Hurry!" said Natasha, her eyes on the cuckoo clock.

The rats quickly modified the trap, turning it into a catapult. They hooked the glider to the ruler with a paper clip.

"I hope you're right about this, Freddy," said Ishbu. He still didn't look happy about the whole thing.

Frederick glanced outside. A flurry of snow met his eyes, so thick that at first he thought someone had drawn lacy curtains across the windows. It was too late to change plans. They'd have to hope for the best.

"Ishbu, you'll sit in front to steer," Frederick told him. "You'll have to hold up the glider's nose so we don't crash."

Ishbu's ears shot up. "Can't you do it?" he squeaked.

Frederick slapped him on the shoulder. "We've come this far, Ishbu. We can't stop now!"

Frederick turned to the others. "Professor, you and Natasha will be in the middle, adding weight to the wings. I'll sit in back and release the bar." He held a letter opener aloft like a spear, ready to cut the twine.

Ishbu and Professor Ratinsky boarded the glider. As Frederick helped Natasha, her whiskers lightly brushed his cheek. "For luck," she whispered.

"Wait!" the professor pointed to his medal hanging on the wall above the desk. "I cannot bear to be thinking of it in paws of Big Cheese."

Frederick scaled the desk and yanked the Benevolence Medal from the wall. He looped the ribbon over his head, and the medal hung across his chest. Then he climbed into the rear of the glider and brandished the letter opener.

"Countdown!" Frederick announced. "Five! Four! Three! Two! One—BLAST OFF!"

He slashed the letter opener downward, slicing the twine with one stroke. The bar snapped forward with tremendous force and hit the erasers. The impact released the glider, and it shot into the air, caught an air current, and sailed out the open window . . . into the swirling snow.

HOW THE MIGHTY FALL

IT WAS A GOOD PLAN. MUCH BETTER THAN most rats could have come up with in similar circumstances. Unfortunately, the weather just wasn't cooperating.

Had it been a calm, sunny day, with a light spring breeze wafting from the mountain, they might have sailed on a downdraft all the way to the village below.

Even in a light snowstorm, with the flakes drifting sideways like the glitter in a glass snow dome, the plan might have worked.

However, what had been a flurry was now a furious blizzard. Perhaps the mightiest blizzard to hit the Swiss Alps in years. Ishbu was completely unable to steer. Gale force winds tore at them, shredding their fragile craft. They spun toward the earth, looping in crazy arcs and arabesques like a daredevil pilot in an air show. Instead of gliding gently into the forest, they headed straight for the knife-edged rocks of the ravine.

Frederick's ears streamed back in the wind. Ishbu's nose burned from the cold. The professor and Natasha clung together.

Their wild ride might have ended in certain death, if an explosive blast of hot air hadn't suddenly shot them up, away from the ravine. Their tattered craft swooped onto the exposed shelf of the glacier. Amazingly, it landed right side up.

The four rats stumbled shakily off the wreck. Frederick shook the snow out of his ears.

"Is everyone okay?" he shouted over the roar of the storm. The other rats nodded. The wind tugged at the mangled glider and blew it away and out of sight.

"It's a miracle we weren't hurt," Natasha shouted back.

"What was that blast?" Frederick asked.

The four rats turned their eyes to the mountain behind them. Orange flames and a plume of smoke erupted where the pet food factory had been.

"I believe factory has exploded," said the professor.

"How?" asked Frederick, wiping a bit of ash out of his eye.

"I warn them," said the professor. He shook his head. "I tell them they need to install better ventilation system. Dust is highly explosive. But will they listen? No! They think I am wanting to use vents to escape!"

"This is end to Big Cheese's plot," said Natasha. "All his bad plans for the world." She rubbed her paws together as though washing them clean of him.

"It's also the end of the Big Cheese!" shouted Ishbu. "Because I bet he'd never leave his headquarters." He grinned. "That's it. It's over. We're safe!" He looked around the glacier field, exposed to the roar of the wind, the snow blowing so hard they could barely see. "Well, maybe not safe, exactly."

"Not to worry," said Frederick. "We'll head downhill into the shelter of those trees." He gestured toward the belt of evergreens below. "Once we get into the village, we can take the train back to France and use the A.B.O.B. network to help us get home. Piece of cake."

"I wish you hadn't mentioned cake," said Ishbu, patting his empty tummy.

They started down the hill. *Back to warmth and civilization! Back to Miss Dove's classroom!* thought Frederick.

That's when they heard the barking.

PURSUIT ON
THE GLACIER

"SNIP!" FREDERICK CRIED IN DISBELIEF.

"And Snarl!" shouted Ishbu.

On the far side of the glacier, coming down from the mountain, they spotted a dogsled, pulled by Snip and Snarl. Mo-Mo crouched on Snarl's back, guiding the way. And on the sled, cracking the whip—who else but the Big Cheese!

"So he did escape!" hollered Ishbu.

"Mo-Mo, too! The powder must have worn off," said Natasha.

"More flaws in formula," murmured Professor Ratinsky.

"What can we do now?" asked Ishbu, clutching his tail. His words streamed away in the howling wind.

"Run!" shouted Frederick.

It was impossible. Four rats—one old and ill, and all decidedly weak with hunger—couldn't outrun a dogsled pulled by two rat terriers. Even a sled slowed by the bulk of an overweight possum. Still, they had to try.

They moved as fast as possible, slipping and sliding across the heavy snow. "If we can make it to the forest, we can hide," panted Frederick. He knew the dogsled could outrun them in the open, but it would have to slow down in the forest.

The green ribbon of the trees beckoned like a finish line at the foot of the glacier. A game of tag—so close and yet so far. Could they make it?

Professor Ratinsky fell on the ice, and Natasha struggled to help him up.

"Go on without me!" he cried.

"I am not leaving you, Papa," said Natasha. Frederick and Ishbu went back and together carried the old rat downhill until their path was blocked by a sign.

Through the blowing snow, Frederick read the bright yellow words.

Closed! Danger!
Gesperrt! Achtung!
Chiuso! Fermé!

What new danger had he dragged his companions into? He paused at the edge of the open ice field while behind them, the dogs closed in. "Stay here!" he ordered. "I have an idea."

Frederick stepped out onto the glacier.

"No!" cried Natasha.

The ice sheet below had been overlaid with the day's fresh snow—heavy, wet, and unstable. Already, deep cracks and crevices were beginning to form.

Frederick hoped the Big Cheese's crew was racing too fast to notice. He hoped the weight of one puny rat wouldn't matter but that the weight of two terriers, one possum, a dogsled, and a show mouse would do the trick.

Step by cautious step, Frederick moved across the ice. At the center of the glacier, he drew himself up to his full height and yelled and waved, daring the Big Cheese to catch him.

The sled was close now, so close that Frederick could see the Big Cheese's alabaster eyes. The horrible baying never stopped, and the dogsled's runners slashed across the snow like knives. In two seconds, they would run him down. His plan wasn't working. . . .

Then, all at once, he heard the crack of doom—and a rumble like ten thousand thunderstorms, seven hundred earthquakes, or fifty tornadoes. Frederick toppled over as the ice field collapsed under the weight of the sled.

Avalanche!

The ground quaked beneath the tsunami of snow. Frederick flailed his paws wildly, as if he were dog-paddling. He heard a startled yelp as the barreling wave crushed the dogsled and its occupants, and then he was flung under the snow. Frederick tumbled around like a pinball. Snow went up his nose and blocked his mouth and ears. He choked on snow. He was drowning in snow. Everything went white.

"WHO GOES SLOWLY..."

FROM THE EDGE OF THE GLACIER, Ishbu had watched as Frederick lured the Big Cheese out onto the fragile ice. Ishbu had heard the booming crack and had seen the snow roll down the mountain, sending a cloud of powdered ice into the air like smoke. He had seen his brother swallowed up by the blinding wall of snow.

"Freddy!" he screamed.

The river of ice poured past the three rats, down the mountain, snapping trees like matchsticks. It slowed and eventually stopped at the foot of the slope, mere meters above the village. The air was incredibly quiet when the avalanche ended, but ice crystals rained down for many minutes afterward. Someone sobbed, and Ishbu realized it was he himself. He buried his face in his paws. Tears ran down his cheeks. His shoulders shook. Kind paws rubbed his back as Natasha, tears streaming down her face as well, tried to comfort him.

Frederick was dead! His brother—the brave rat, the educated rat, the lover of adventure, the hero —had perished trying to help others, trying to thwart the evil plans of the Big Cheese.

Ishbu scrubbed his eyes with his paws and took a shuddering sniff. He tiptoed out onto the ravaged glacier. He wanted to mark Frederick's grave somehow, to leave some memorial.

A flicker of pink caught his eye.

Ishbu peered at the mounded snow. It couldn't be! The very tip of a rat tail? And it moved!

"Freddy!" Grabbing the tail, Ishbu pulled with all his strength. It was no good. Frederick was buried too deeply.

"Give me a paw!" Ishbu hollered. Natasha and the professor scampered out and frantically began to dig. At last, they freed the buried rat. Frederick was limp and icy cold. Ignoring the wind and snow, Ishbu cradled his brother in his arms.

Frederick's eyelids fluttered. He blinked at his friends. "Did—did it work?" he asked.

Ishbu nodded. He couldn't stop grinning. "You did it! We really won this time!"

Ishbu looked around. The snow still fell heavily. They were miles from anywhere, stranded somewhere in the Swiss Alps, still without food, water, shelter . . .

And now they could see—on the other side of a crevasse, angrily shaking his fist—the Big Cheese! They couldn't hear his words above the howling wind. But the meaning was clear.

There was no sign of the dogsled, the terriers, or Mo-Mo.

Ishbu looked at his brother, and Frederick looked at him. They both grinned. None of it mattered. Not the Big Cheese, not the snow, not the gnawing hunger pangs. They were together—Ishbu and Frederick, Frederick and Ishbu. Brothers and friends to the end.

"He'll have a hard time getting out of here without the help of the Bilgewater Brigade," said Ishbu. Frederick nodded. They turned their backs on the possum.

"*Chi va piano, va sano e va lontano,*" said Professor Ratinsky. "An old Italian proverb: Who goes slowly, goes safely and goes far."

Ishbu laughed. "You mean 'Slow and steady wins the race'!"

The four rats clasped paws and—step by careful step—they started down the mountain.

Epilogue:
HOME, SWEET HOME

Be it ever so humble, there's no place like home.
—John Howard Payne

HOME!

THE RATS WERE BACK IN MISS Dove's cage, back in the fifth-grade classroom at Wilberforce Harrison Elementary School.

Frederick arched his spine to get the kinks out. He felt fully recovered now from his ordeal on the glacier. They had retraced their steps across Switzerland, first taking the train and postal bus to Madeleine's burrow in France. Then Madeleine had helped them stow away on an airplane traveling to San Francisco, and from there it was a hop, skip, and a jump to Miss Dove's room.

They had arrived late at night and scuttled through an open window. The classroom had been empty. The lights had been off, but the cage door had stood open. Water, food, and fresh bedding were waiting for them—as if Miss Dove had known they would return.

Frederick cracked a walnut and offered half to

Natasha, noticing how the sparkle had returned to her eyes.

"Explain it to me again," said Ishbu, chewing a carrot stick.

"Frederick was able to save us because he read Danger sign," Natasha told him. "He knew conditions were ripe for avalanche."

"As I always say: never underestimate good education," added the professor. A bit of white marshmallow stuck to his whiskers, and he licked it off. He looked stronger already.

"You know what, Freddy?" said Ishbu. "Now that we're back, I'm going to learn to read, too."

The four rats feasted until the first streaks of daylight filtered through the blinds. When they had eaten their fill of marshmallows, walnuts, and slightly bruised grapes, Natasha put her paw on Frederick's. "My father and I can never be thanking you and your brother enough," she said. "But here is small token of our gratitude." She handed him a package wrapped in tissue.

"Where did you get that?" asked Ishbu. Natasha merely smiled.

Frederick tore off the wrapping to reveal a small red object, just the right size for a rat. "Gosh!" said Frederick. "A genuine Swiss army knife!"

"So you can be opening your cage anytime," said Natasha.

"Thanks!" said Frederick. He examined the knife. In addition to a tiny blade, it had a nail file (always practical), a pair of delicate scissors, miniature tweezers, and an ivory toothpick. "How handy," he said, beaming.

"Just the thing for world explorer!" Natasha fluttered her long eyelashes, and the tips of Frederick's ears turned pink.

"And I have something for your father," Frederick said. He handed Professor Ratinsky the Benevolence Medal that he'd worn since recovering it from the Big Cheese.

The professor's eyes crinkled behind his glasses. He took the medal and twisted it in both paws. Two halves slid apart, and the medal opened like a locket, revealing a secret compartment. Frederick and the others leaned close as the professor pulled out a scrap of paper.

"What is it?" Natasha asked.

The professor unfolded the paper. Cramped writing covered both sides—numbers, letters, figures—a mathematical equation, or . . .

"The formula!" breathed Frederick.

"Big Cheese had it in his grasp all the time," said Professor Ratinsky, nodding. "And he never knew."

Then the professor ripped the paper into shreds. He scattered the pieces among the torn newspapers lining the cage. "Gone for good," he said. "Out of the reach of villains." He tapped his forehead. "Only exists in here now."

"But what if the Big Cheese comes after you again?" said Ishbu.

"We go home to Russia. We have many friends there. Big Cheese will not be finding us . . . we hope," said Natasha. She glanced out the window. "It is nearly dawn. We must be leaving. We do not want to surprise your Miss Dove with four rats instead of two."

The rats scampered out of the cage and across the floor. They swarmed up the radiator to the window ledge. They perched on the sill, looking out at the gray morning.

"*Dasvidanja*, dear friends. Good-bye!" said Professor Ratinsky, shaking paws heartily with the two brothers. He climbed out and waited in the flower bed.

Natasha gave Ishbu a hug. He hugged her back, all traces of distrust gone.

Then Natasha drew close to Frederick. Her cinnamon scent made his head swim. She lightly brushed his whiskers with her own, thrilling him down to the tip of his tail.

"Will I ever see you again?" asked Frederick sadly.

"The world is small when two hearts meet," whispered Natasha. Tears glittered on her lashes, and

Frederick brushed them away. "Remember," she said, "you have your knife to be leaving whenever you want."

Natasha joined her father outside, and they scurried across the playground. Frederick watched until they were out of sight.

Frederick turned a half circle in his cage, taking in the torn maps and papers covering the floor (including the shredded formula), the comfortable shoe box bed, the water bottle, and the food dish.

In a few hours Miss Dove and the children would bustle in, and lessons would start. Once again Miss Dove would enchant the class with tales of faraway places, legends of heroes and heroines, and stories of remarkable discoveries—never imagining that a world explorer (or two!) was right there in her classroom.

Ishbu would learn to read, and Frederick had a new goal, too: to master a foreign language! Maybe Chinese or Spanish or Russian . . . How useful it would be—the next time they went adventuring!

Author's Note

As a teacher, I've kept rats as class pets. Two of those rats were named Frederick and Ishbu. Frederick was a lilac rat, and Ishbu was a hooded rat. They really were brothers. As far as I know, neither rat learned to read, although I'm sure they had plenty of opportunities.

I love writing the Frederick and Ishbu books because my research turns up so many interesting tidbits. Here are just a few of the things I learned while researching *The Case of the Purloined Professor*.

Show Mice

"Fancy mice" and "fancy rats" are the terms used for mice and rats that have been bred for show. The hobby started in China and became very popular in Victorian England. Today, there are rat and mouse clubs throughout the world. There are international competitions, although most contestants don't travel to them in private jets! The competitions are similar to dog shows, with the mice and rats judged on conformation (body symmetry), color, and markings. Like other show animals, fancy mice and rats are bred for certain characteristics.

Mousetrap Catapults

You can build a working catapult out of a mousetrap. This is a great science-fair project for demonstrating simple machines and physics concepts such as force and gravity. Also, it's just plain fun. You can launch Ping-Pong balls or marshmallows. Plans are available on the Internet. Although Frederick used a rat trap, you should use a mousetrap instead, as rat traps are dangerous even if you aren't a rat. You will need adult supervision.

Robert Burns

Robert Burns is considered the national poet of Scotland. He was born in Alloway, Scotland, in 1759. He grew up on a farm and was mostly self-educated. Among his most famous poems are "Auld Lang Syne" (sung on New Year's Eve) and "Bannockburn," the unofficial national anthem of Scotland, which I used as the lyrics for the Highland Badger Fling. He died in 1796 at the age of thirty-seven. He continues to be celebrated by Scots, poetry lovers, and English teachers everywhere.

Edgar Allan Poe

Edgar the raven is named after Edgar Allan Poe, a famous American author. Poe was born in Boston, Massachusetts, in 1809. He is considered the father of detective fiction. His stories and poems, which remain popular today, are known for their creepy and mysterious atmosphere. Among his best-loved works are the short story "The Purloined Letter" and the poem "The Raven." He died in 1849.

Badgers

Badgers are one of the most popular wild animals in the United Kingdom. They live in family groups called clans, which is also the word used in Scotland for large, extended families. They build dens, called setts, consisting of networks of tunnels. *Sett* is also the term for the patterns of tartan (commonly called plaid in the United States) used to identify clans in Scotland. The old Scottish word for *badger* is *brock*, which I used as a name for one of the A.B.O.B. badgers.

The names Duncan and MacDuff come from the play *Macbeth* by William Shakespeare, which takes place in Scotland in a setting like Aberglen Castle.

San Francisco Chinese New Year Parade

One of the most famous parades in the world takes place in San Francisco's Chinatown. The parade celebrates the Chinese New Year, which (according to the Chinese calendar) can occur anytime between January and the end of February.

The grand finale of the parade is the procession of the 201-foot-long golden dragon known as Gum Lung.

More than one hundred people carry the huge head and the fabric tail that billows and undulates as they dance through the streets. Although I have seen the parade, I didn't notice if any rats hitched rides on the dancers' feet.

JUDY COX lives with her husband and son in Ontario, Oregon. Her first novel in the Frederick and Ishbu series, *The Mystery of the Burmese Bandicoot*, and *The Case of the Purloined Professor*, bring the wit and wisdom of her popular chapter books and picture books (including *Don't Be Silly, Mrs. Millie!*) to middle grade readers and draw on her own experience as a teacher.